THE GREAT GETAWAY

by

Robbie Moffat

PALM TREE PUBLISHING

PALM TREE PUBLISHING
Paisley, Scotland Pa1 1TJ

© Robbie Moffat 2014-2019

First published in digital form NOVEMBER 2014
First published in paperback JANUARY 2109

Typeset: Verdana 8pt

ISBN-10: 0 907282568
ISBN-13: 978-0907282563

INTRODUCTION

There are some great stories that get told time and time again. There are other great stories forgotten about, buried in the history books, lost in time, no longer remembered.

The Great Getaway lives in the literature of Scott and Stevenson, the songs of Burns, and the national conscience of Scotland. The living landscape of the story has changed little since the time of its taking place. The place names, the clan names, these resonate through modern Scottish life.

There can be few Scots who have not sung one of the countless songs that celebrates the hero of our story. He is a remarkable romantic figure who changed British society and who by his deeds pushed the Union of Scotland and England into its empire days. Without the success of his single minded purpose of restoring his family's fortunes, and the consequences of that success that turned to apparent failure, the burgeoning idea of Scotland and England being a single unified nation, may not have succeeded.

In the Highlands resides the noblest part of of Scottish nature. This is revealed to our hero time and time again; honesty, integrity, loyalty, a belief in charity, humanity, and a willingness to assist when the might of the state is determined to do the underdog down.

In our story, the underdog is Charles Edward Stuart, better remembered as Bonnie Prince Charlie. Starting as the story of the biggest manhunt ever mounted, by trial and tribulation, it transforms into the greatest escape story in British history.

DEDICATION

This book is dedicated to everyone in Scotland who is proud of our nation.

> While the past contains days of hope,
> times of joy, lost summers of plenty -
> the path before us goes over the horizon,
> where those we know, never come back.

1

Mist. The sound of hooves.

Sound of pistol shots. Muskets. Cannon.

The morning of 16th APRIL 1746, Drummossie Moor, Culloden.

Prince Charles Edward Stuart, twenty-five, handsome, fair complexion, hair in ringlets, wild eyed is distressed. He is flanked by Irishman Quartermaster General Colonel John O'Sullivan, forty-six, a Kerry man in the French blue army uniform; Captain Felix O'Neil, forty-two, also from Kerry in the red and green of the Hibernia of Spain uniform; Captain Alexander MacLeod, twenty-six, aide-de-camp, Highland uniform; and Ned Burke, fifty, MacLeod's man servant from Edinburgh.

They are all mounted and in disarray.

Colonel O'Sullivan is shouting above the din. "The battle is lost!"

"I will not leave my army!"

The Prince's horse is shot from under him. He goes down with the horse.

O'Neil and MacLeod dismount to help the Prince.

"Ned! A mount for the Prince!" Captain MacLeod pulls on the reins of the Prince's dying horse.

Ned rides off.

Captain O'Neil helps the Prince to his feet.

O'Sullivan is shouting. "We must retire now!" He fires a pistol at the enemy advancing on their position.

Ned arrives with a horse for the Prince.

"Mount, sir!" O'Neil urges the Prince to place his hand on the saddle.

The Prince does as he is told. Ned holds the reins.

MacLeod and O'Neil remount.

O'Sullivan is hacking at a Redcoat with his cutlass. "Ride!"

They turn their mounts. A dozen Redcoats besiege them.

The Prince, Ned and O'Sullivan fight their way free and gallop off.

O'Neil and MacLeod fight rear guard – break free and follow after the Prince.

The sun is breaking through on to the black waters of Loch Ness.

There is a trickle of fleeing MacDonald's and camp followers hurrying along the Wade Road.

Two riders in Highland Army colours come galloping over the hill above the road. They rein their mounts.

Colonel Elcho, twenty-four, in Life-Guard uniform, is badly wounded in the shoulder. Accompanying him is Sir Thomas Sheridan, seventy, the Prince's tutor.

Elcho is in severe pain "The Prince must get himself to France."

Sheridan, out of breath from the hard ride, is angry. "You do not know Charles Edward Stuart. I've taught him never to give up! Never!"

"You have neglected your duties, Sheridan, with your Irish flattery, and your deferment to the Prince! We Scotsmen have risked our lives for his cause! For what end???"

Sheridan gives Elcho a disdainful look. Elcho is dismissive of the old tutor's attitude. He turns to face the approach of five riders - the Prince, O'Sullivan, O'Neil, MacLeod and Ned.

The Prince is agitated. "Colonel Elcho! Is that the main road to Fort William???

"Aye, sir. Clogged with MacDonalds fleeing to save their own skins!"

The Prince turns to his aide-de-camp. "MacLeod! Find General Murray and bring him to me."

"Where will I find you, sir?"

"Lochiel's house!"

Captain MacLeod addresses his servant. "I trust the Prince to you, Ned!"

MacLeod swings his horse around, gallops off.

The remaining party ride on at speed.

There is an air of uneasy quiet as the Prince's party approach the large mansion of Clan Cameron. They halt fifty yards from the house.

"I'll take a look, sir." O'Neil nudges his horse forward, enters the courtyard.

There are no signs of habitation.

O'Neil waves to the Prince's party to ride up to the house.

Donald Cameron of Lochiel, fifty-five, lies in his kitchen wounded in the legs, attended by two battle-worn Cameron Retainers.

The Prince's party enters with haste, searching for food.

"Lochiel!"

Lochiel props himself up on his elbows. "Get away to France, Charles. Speak to King Louie. Raise a new army and come back again!"

"I have to speak with General Murray." The Prince is still taken up by the burden of leadership matters.

"Murray! The man's the ruin of us all."

Sheridan cuts in. "That's enough, Cameron. Remember who you're speaking with."

"I favour anyone who can advise me bluntly, Thomas."

Elcho gives Sheridan a glare.

Outside, Ned is keeping watch from a small mound.

In the distance are a company of mounted Redcoats.

He turns and runs into the house.

Ned enters the kitchen in a panic. "Dragoons are coming down the glen!"

"How far off?" O'Sullivan is loading his pistols.

"A mile at most!"

The men hurriedly gather their belongings and weapons.

Lochiel, up on his feet, is helped by his Retainers. "Ned. Take the Prince and the Colonel to my brother Archie's!"

He is using a sword to support himself. He addresses the Prince. "You are in mortal danger. I beg you to leave now."

Prince Charles realises the urgency of the moment. "Adieu, my friend." They embrace.

Elcho gets up to make his farewell. He collapses from loss of blood.

"Captain O'Neil! Help Colonel Elcho. Your highness, go, please!"

Ned, Charles and O'Sullivan take Lochiel's advice and depart hastily.

Lochiel is resigned to the events. "Gentlemen ... my house is about to be burnt to the ground ..." He picks up a bottle of wine and a loaf of bread " ... take what you need. There will be few comforts left to us when we are hiding in the woods."

Prince Charles, O'Sullivan, and Ned are once more on horseback.

They are picking their way along a narrow mountain track. The mountains cram in on both sides. The going is steep. Ned is the least able horseman and lags behind.

O'Sullivan is concerned. "Keep your hand tight on the reins, Ned."

"I am Colonel!" Ned looks down at the hundred-foot drop over a cliff edge.

"And don't look down!"

Ned mutters to himself "Now he tells me. Those two have been riding horses since they were bairns. Come on, Ned, show them that an Embra boy is no scared of heights."

Over the shoulder of the track dropping away ahead, a small house reveals itself nestled in the lee of the glen.

Doctor Cameron's parlour in the ben of the house is small but exceedingly comfortable in the Highland fashion. The Prince is sitting before the open fire with a blanket draped around him. O'Sullivan is resting in a rocking chair. Ned, for his sins as a servant, is in the next room that doubles as the scullery at the back of the house that leads to the outside byre.

Doctor Archibald Cameron of Lochiel is filling a pipe bowl with tobacco. O'Sullivan is standing reading Cameron's framed credentials on the mantelpiece – University of Edinburgh studies, with further medical certificates from the Universities of Paris and Leiden.

"Will you take a smoke, your highness?" Cameron hands Charles a clay pipe.

"I'm not accustomed to it, Doctor Cameron."

"Its a gentleman's custom in these parts."

"When I came to this country, it was my view to do all I could for you. Now, it is you who are doing for me."

Cameron lights the pipe for the Prince.

"Lets make what cheer we can, sir. A glass of port?"

Charles sucks on the pipe, nods.

Colonel Sullivan sits down. "You have some terrible mountains in this part, Archie?"

"Aye, some of the highest in Scotland."

"Not fit to take an army over?"

"It would be suicide."

The Prince feels left out of the conversation. "How far is it to the coast?"

"A day and a half. You'll no be getting horses over these hills. Its by foot or nothing."

He hands Charles, then O'Sullivan a glass of port. "I remember when you landed at Glenfinnan, I was with Lochiel when we marched in, the pipes skirling. What a day that was. When Tullibardine unfurled the standard, my heart went up with my bonnet."

"I'm sorry for what has occurred since."

"That day was the grandest of my life. This day is grand too for having your royal highness in my house."

"Thank you, Archie."

Charles raises a toast. "To my father King James. And to Doctor Cameron for sheltering us at this difficult time."

"The honour is mine, your highness."

They drink.

The sun is just up over the hills. Alexander MacLeod comes over the last rise and rides up to Doctor Cameron's house.

O'Sullivan walks to greet him as he approaches.

"What news, Alex?"

"Bad news, John. Cumberland has butchered our wounded!"

"Jesus." O'Sullivan is perplexed by this information. "All of them?"

"Every last man and boy."

MacLeod dismounts.

"Have any of our men escaped?"

"About fifteen hundred. They are waiting at Ruthven for orders."

"Is Murray with them?"

MacLeod shakes his head. He pushes a letter on O'Sullivan.

O'Sullivan takes the letter. It is addressed to the Prince.

O'Sullivan puts the letter into his tunic. "Not a word about the butchery."

MacLeod nods, leads his horse, walks with O'Sullivan slowly towards the house.

MacLeod and Ned are a little way off.

The Prince sits on a wood chopping block, eating curd from a bowl.

O'Sullivan is opening Murray's letter. He quickly scans it. His face drops.

"Read away, John."

"Its impudent!" He crumples the letter, throws it away.

"Colonel! We must have the substance of his news..."

O'Sullivan picks the letter up, straightens out the creases, reads aloud. "Your Royal Highness. I can bear my own family's ruin without a grudge, but it was highly wrong to have set up the royal standard without the aid of France." O'Sullivan takes a deep breath. "For the defeat yesterday, I blame O'Sullivan for incompetence, and your RH for giving him unwarranted responsibility!"

O'Sullivan breaks off. "The man is insufferable! Not one criticism of the MacDonalds turning tail before the battle."

"Read on, John."

O'Sullivan shakes the letter, clears his throat. "We may have defeated the enemy but the day before the battle the soldiers only got one biscuit apiece. They were famished." Breaks off. "Because of this fool's tactics!"

"Please. Finish the letter".

"Since our retreat from Derby, I always told your RH I had no design to continue in the army. I hope your RH will now accept my decommission!"

O'Sullivan is livid. "The coward has resigned!"

The Prince continues to eat his curd.

O'Sullivan is pacing. "He still has fifteen hundred men under his command!"

The Prince puts down his bowl, looks up. "General Murray has played his part."

O'Sullivan draws him a look. "So its over?"

"For the time being..." Charles gets up. "Mister MacLeod. Tell every man to seek his own safety. Find Lochiel and tell him to get his party to Borrodale where we will board a ship for France."

MacLeod is visibly disappointed. He bows.

"Give me a few hundred men, Charlie, and I'll make these hills ours till you come back from France."

"No! We are done."

O'Sullivan starts to plead with Charles. "Your royal highness...."

"I am the Commander in Chief!" The Prince goes into the house.

O'Sullivan rips up the letter.

Ned holds MacLeod's horse as he mounts.

"See you in Borrodale."

He rides off.

Ned joins O'Sullivan who is sitting on the chopping block looking at his boots.

"We're in the mire, aren't we, Colonel?"

"Up to our chins."

"Can I speak out of place, sir?"

"Speak freely, Ned."

"His personage sticks out like a bonfire in the dark. How are we going to hide his radiance from the Redcoats?"

O'Sullivan looks at Ned as though he is stupid. "Disguise, Ned."

"Oh aye? Disguise him as what?"

The mountains loom into the sky ahead.

On foot, Archie Cameron and O'Sullivan are leading the small party. Charles and Ned in the rear have exchanged clothes. Charles looks uncomfortable in his new attire.

"These clothes are giving me the itch."

"I'd rather have the itch than be in these stockings, your highness."

"Why, Ned, if only you'd been so well dressed carrying sedan chairs in Edinburgh. You would have made your fortune."

"I know my place, sir. Carrying sedans is a muddy affair. Out in all weathers. I've trodden many a road, but none as nasty as this."

He starts to whistle the *The Young Highland Rover*.

"Come, Ned. Where in Edinburgh would you get a view like this?

Ned stops whistling, takes a good look at the wild mountains.

"Well, I'm quite partial to the view from Edinburgh Castle looking towards Leith."

"That's because it contains all the vices of the world."

"You've got me there, sir. You know this servant Ned through and through. But looking at you, now that you are in my shoes, I think you as my servant are thinking of the vices of the world."

Charles laughs loudly.

Archie and O'Sullivan look back.

"Is that man always so damned familiar with his royal highness?"

"Too much so. Ned Burke's been to Derby and back with us. If he keeps the Prince humoured then we are to be thankful."

The light is fading. The party of four descend into the valley, enter a wood.

Charles flops down against a tree.

"This is a miserable living, John."

"Aye, it is, sir, but when we reach the ship, we'll be well fed and wined."

"What I would give for Parma ham and a bottle of Piedmont Barolo."

Ned rubs his lips. "I'd settle for bread and cheese."

"You see, John. Ned has brought us back to our situation. Until we leave Scotland, we must expect to be thwarted of comfort."

"Aye, sir. Master or servant. They've all the same tastes. Tis a dull life for the tongue in Scotland."

Charles is sleeping.

Archie Cameron arrives with Angus MacEachine, twenty-two, in highland soldier uniform, carrying a doctor's bag.

"Angus the surgeon, sir. I got away from Culloden and only just arrived home. Is the Prince wounded?"

"No, he's just foot sore."

"Have you any injuries, sir?"

O'Sullivan shake his head.

Doctor Cameron makes ready to take his leave. "Angus will take you on to Borrodale."

"Are you not journeying on with us, Archie?

Archie offers O'Sullivan's his hand.

"I'm going back to my house in case some villains ransack it. And your horses. I'll have to get ride them off."

"The Redcoats will never find your cottage."

"No, but some of the Highland Militia know where I live and might to take it on themselves to visit. The whole country is turned upside down. Nothing can be taken for granted. God bless you all."

He departs briskly.

Ned who has been listening is anxious for his own safety. "Should I wake the Prince?"

"Let him be. Its his first good sleep for a month."

"Aye. He's a wee bit touchy when he's no had his full sleep."

The three men settle in the wood - wrap themselves in their plaids.

The Prince's party emerges from a wood onto the shore.

Beyond across the water are Skye and Eigg. The high mountain on Rhum is lost in low cloud.

Angus leads Charles, O'Sullivan and Ned along the shore. They are ever watchful for the enemy.

"This is where I landed last year? Loch nan Uamh?

"Aye. It is."

Ahead is the house of Angus MacDonald of Borrodale.

O'Neil, Sheridan, Elcho and Captain MacLeod come out the house – see the Prince. They haste to greet him.

Sheridan is on intimate terms with his charge. "My boy.... You're safe." He embraces Charles like a father. The Prince has grown out of the relationship but acquiesces to the old man's warm welcome.

The Prince "Where's Lochiel? Felix?"

Captain O'Neil shakes his head. "He couldn't walk, sir. He's still holed up near his house."

"And the enemy? Are they close to us?"

Captain MacLeod interjects. "Cumberland is set up at Fort Augustus."

O'Neil is hungry to keep up the fight. "With a few hundred of the boys, sir, we could cut his army to pieces."

"That is my counsel." O'Sullivan still has the fight left in him too. "Pin them down at Fort Augustus so they can't relieve the garrison at Fort William."

Colonel Elcho, now heavily bandage, is defeatist. "To what end? They'd burn every village in retaliation? Cumberland is a brute." He appeals to the Prince. "Its a lost cause, sir."

Charles is discomforted by Elcho's bitterness.

"Don't listen to the Colonel, sir. He's just a Lowland lawyer. He's done playing soldiers and wants to go home!"

"Hold your tongue, O'Neil." Elcho coughs blood.

"Well, Charlie?" O'Sullivan is pushing for a decision.

The Prince is unable to think clearly. He is still numbed by the scale of his reversed fortunes.

"I need more intelligence, John." It is obvious he is fatigued. "Any news of our ship, Alex?"

"No, sir."

There is an awkward silence. O'Sullivan and O'Neil exchange a look that confirms that they know their advice has been ignored.

Sheridan defuses the silence. "We must get you out of those rags, boy...." He guides Charles towards the house.

Ned buttonholes O'Sullivan. "Colonel. Can I have my clothes back, sir? I'd rather wear my rags than be dressed like a cockerel to be shot at by the Redcoats."

O'Sullivan puts his arm around Ned's shoulders. "Are you not ready to go up in the world, Ned?"

"No, sir. I am a humble servant. Please don't try to change me, I will resist."

Ned scurries into the cottage.

Inside the house, Sheridan leads the Prince to a table. Ned enters hastily, sits with the Prince.

Charles points out the food spread before them - lamb, fish, cheese, and butter. "See, Ned, you must expect more from life!"

"I concede, master. I never expected such delights in such a modest abode."

Captain MacLeod taps Ned on the shoulder "Out..."

"Leave him be, Alexander. Since Michele was captured, he has been of good service to me."

MacLeod gives Ned a look.

Ned is sympathetic. "Och, master, your old servant Michele. He was a fine old Italian gentleman."

"Tis a tragedy, Ned. I have lost the family servant. My father will be sore."

"Had he been with you long, master?"

"Before I was born. Michele managed the escape of my mother from Austria so they could marry."

Catriona MacDonald of Borrodale, the wife of the house is brought forward by Angus. She is carrying a bundle.

"Lady Catriona. We met last year when I landed with your husband."

She nods "Aye, we did, your highness." She opens the bundle on the table and pulls out a plaid suit. Charles picks it up the suit.

"This is a fine garment. Its MacDonald plaid?"

Angus interjects. "My father-in-law's."

The Prince is reminded of his old supporter. "Is Borrodale home yet?"

Angus shakes his head. "We fear him lost, sir."

O'Neil enters. "We've just hear that Cumberland has sent a detachment south to cut us off the road to Fort William. We may have to take a ship from Skye.

The Prince gets up, starts to pace about.

Sheridan tires to pacify him. "Rest, Charles."

"Not now, Thomas."

"Bad news is not best digested with bad humour."

The Prince is curt with him. "This is not Rome."

"No it is not, Charles. I've known you all of your life and I know when you are likely to make rash decisions."

"Are you chastising me?"

"I'm your natural uncle. I am trying to offer advice."

"Advice, Thomas? Do you think we should we take the fight to Cumberland again?"

"As Colonel Elcho said. Tis a lost cause. You tried your best. It is not to be. Lets go home before we cause more misery and suffering."

Charles winces.

"Surely that is what you want to hear, Charles?"

"You are right, Thomas. I'm of little use here. The sooner I gain an audience with Louis, the sooner I can return with an army."

Charles, dressed in his new plaid suit is alone with his thoughts. He is looking out over the water at the narrow expanse of water that separates the mainland from Skye.

Donald MacLeod, a small stooped man of sixty-eight, approaches him.

The Prince turns.

"I am Donald MacLeod the boatman. May it please your highness ... at your service."

"I am out of sorts, Donald. My ship has not come." Charles paces in an agitated manner. "I'm told that you are the finest seaman in the Hebrides."

Donald is abashed at the compliment.

"I must leave from here for my own safety, so I throw myself into your hands."

Donald is dumbfounded. "I am an old man. I can do very little for myself these days."

"Nonsense. You look fine and well. I want you to deliver me to Skye." He points across the water.

"I don't understand? To who, your highness?"

"To MacDonald of Sleat or MacLeod of MacLeod?"

Donald turns indignant. "I will not do it, sir, though you hang me for it."

Charles is incredulous.

"Does your excellency not know? These chiefs have played the rogue with you! And you trust them for all that? Naw, I will nae do it."

Charles is visibly agitated. "Why are you so cold with them?"

"They are loyal Hanoverians! MacDonald and MacLeod have their own militia out looking for you on Skye." Donald points to the Cuillins.

"But I am here?"

"Your only hope is to leave for the Long Island, your excellency, afore they cross and find you here."

"What about the British navy?"

Donald is gleeful. "Gone to St. Kilda. A whisper in the right ear, another in a tavern, and in an hour, thirty ships, three regiments, up anchor to yon faraway outpost."

"They think I am on St. Kilda?"

"Do you see a single mast, your highness? The Minch is clear of ships and Redcoats all the way from Lewis to Barra."

Charles clasps Donald by the hand. "You have given me hope! Can you carry me across tonight?"

"Young Borrodale's brother has a good boat with a mast."

Charles sees something in Donald's look. "He was at Culloden?"

"Aye. Murdered in cold blood, as he lay wounded. My own son saw it."

Charles is confused by the information Donald has given him.

Donald passes over it. "There's a gale on the way. Its not a night for going to sea."

"But I must cross tonight … you said so yourself."

Donald recalls his own words and the immediacy of the situation the Prince is in. "I'll prepare the boat, your highness." Donald curtsies and leaves.

Charles clasps his hands together, makes a silent prayer. In silhouette, he is a lone figure on a hostile shore.

The boat contains six MacLeod Boatman. Donald is making last minute preparations, stowing provisions, checking that all the oars are seaworthy.

There is a ragtag assembly of exhausted Highland army soldiers scattered along the beach.

The Prince, O'Sullivan, O'Neil and Ned are on the shoreline with Sheridan, Elcho, Angus and MacDonald Retainers. O'Neil has his hand on the shoulder of Young Donald, fifteen, Donald MacLeod's son.

"You say that the Redcoats bayoneted Young Borrodale after the battle?"

Young Donald is pained to tell the story. "It was for sport. They are butchers!"

Charles is visibly shocked.

"They rounded up the wounded from the nearby houses, brought them back to the field, and shot them. Angus saw it too!"

Angus looks up from dressing Elcho's wound. He nods.

"How old are you?"

"Fifteen, your highness."

"My God. Your boy should be in school, Donald."

"Aye, he should."

"I left the Grammar School in Inverness, got myself a dirk and pistol to join your army." Young Donald has his hand on his pistol.

"Why give up your studies for this terrible life?"

"I want to see the end of German Geordie. I want you as my king."

"My father James is king, Donald?"

"He's over the water, sir. You are here."

Old Donald intervenes. He speaks in Gaelic. "Get in the boat, Donnie."

"Yes, father." Young Donald does as he is told.

Captain O'Neil throws in his opinion. "The boy's lucky. Others have been stripped, flogged, and paraded naked through the streets of Inverness."

This is also new information for the Prince. "On Prince William's orders?

"Aye. We have had a report that prisoners are being starved to death."

Charles puts his head in his hands. "William is my cousin. He's the same age as myself. It cannot be true?"

O'Sullivan is matter of fact. "Cumberland is a nasty bloated creature. He has a talent for military matters, but his tactics are as crude as his methods. I had first hand sight of that at Dettingen two years ago. Now, he seems to have perfected his taste for murder."

Donald MacLeod shouts. "Sirs, we must be away or miss the tide!"

Charles turns to Sheridan. "I am loathe to leave you behind, Thomas."

"I have no stomach for small boats, Charles. I will wait here for the ship, and if it comes, direct it to the Long Island enroute to France."

Elcho kisses the Princes hand.

"I regret you are not well enough to come with us, David."

"No, Charles. But we have had a good run, have we not?"

Charles does not answer the question. He smiles.

"Mister MacLeod! When the ship comes, they have to take onboard all of our officers who assemble on the beach. Is that clear?"

"Aye, sir. And please have a messenger send word to me when you are safely across."

"Have no fears on that, Alex. You will be the first to have the news of my situation."

The Prince gets into the boat. A piper plays *The Eight Men of Moidart* as the boat is pushed out.

Charles looking back extends his arm in salute to the small crowd of friends and soldiers scattered on the beach.

The Men on shore return it.

Donald hoists the sail as the boatmen pull in their oars. The sea is choppy. Charles holds on to the side of the boat.

Ragged clouds hurry across the sky. There is a gale blowing from the north. A tremendous sea is running. Under a rag of canvas, the boat is pressed down to the gunnels.

Donald takes a long look over the foaming water. The boat is making a foot to the lee for every two she forges ahead. The sail is raised and lowered as they rise from a trough or go over a breaking crest.

Charles, O'Sullivan, O'Neil, and Ned are hanging over the side - being sick. A Boatman is fighting hard to trim the sail. The other Boatmen and Young Donald are constantly baling.

Lighting flashes. THUNDER.

A great sea strikes the stern. The Prince holds on to a cross-plank for dear-life. A savage wave breaks across him - knocks him flat against the side of the boat.

O'Sullivan and O'Neil rise to help. They are swept off their feet. All three are thrown upon each other.

The boat makes a loud CRACK sound. The boom swings over their heads - swings back on its tack.

The boatmen themselves are alarmed. The sail is dropped.

The Prince picks himself up. "There is no hurt!"

The Boatmen pull on their oars with zeal.

Donald looks ahead. "White water! Rory?"

Boatman Rory MacLeod at the bow strains through the lashing rain. "Its Benbecula!"

The rest are stiffened and too benumbed with cold to respond.

It is the dawn of the April 27th as the boat pulls towards the safety of the bay at Roisinish, Benbecula

Donald, at the helm, steers the boat through the rocky inlet of small islands and outcrops of seaweed-draped protrusions.

The boat drops sail as it approaches a narrow strip of shingle beach that has been cleared of rocks by generations of fishermen. The sea is foaming on the pebbled shore as the bottom of the boat grinds onto a semblance of land.

The wind is blowing fiercely as they disembark and they struggle to keep their feet on the moving shoreline as they haul the boat out the water.

Donald points towards a shieling sitting on a ledge of grass high above the high water mark. The Prince and his party, with their heads to the wind, battle to get off the beach. They are weary and exhausted.

A Herdsman emerges from the shieling. He sees the strangers coming up the beach, and in fear, makes off inland.

The interior of the bothy is bare. The floor is hard baked mud soon made soft and dirty by the party of seafarers dripping with brine. The Prince's party, the Boatmen, Donald and Young Donald, drop wearily; spread themselves across the floor where there is space. The only source of light is from the hole in the roof.

They are removing their wet clothes. They are all talking at once, wondering at the miracle of having survived the gale.

"In my sixty-eight years, I never had such a crossing!"

"I'd rather face cannons and muskets than be in a storm like that again." The Prince is laughing at his own misfortune.

Everyone is grateful to be alive.

"How was that for you, young Donald?"

"I was more frightened than I was at the battle, your highness."

They are all in agreement.

"Come, come, Donnie let us get a fire made. You see the condition the Prince is in."

Charles is wet through, but not any seeking special treatment. "Whom was that man running off?"

Donald MacLeod is gestures to the belongings scattered about the hut. "The shepherd who's here for the summer grazing."

"Will he give alarm?"

"He'll run and tell the land owner about us. Ranald Macdonald's house is five miles that way at Nunton"

"This is Chief MacDonald's land?"

"Aye, it is. You'll know Clanranald then, sir?

"Yes, Donald I do. His son Ranald was a great friend to me in Paris."

"Until he ran off at Culloden." O'Sullivan is making it clear that Ranald is not in favour with the Prince. "His father is no friend of the Prince's."

Donald removes his jerkin. "Tis unfortunate then, so it is, sir, that the wind brought us to Benbecula, rather than Lochmaddy or Barra where your cause is better supported."

"It is, Donald, but when you are a Prince, even your enemies can be your friends in times of trouble."

An old iron pot is bubbling over a fire. Ned is removing butter and cheese from a small wooden chest. "There's little enough for all of us, sir." He indicates the Boatmen.

Donald is stoical. "My men are happy to be here hungry or not."

The Prince opens a purse and removes some coins. "Nonsense. Go shoot yourself a cow." He hands the coins to Donald.

"I don't think I'll be doing that."

"Here is the payment for the herdsman. I command it."

"Tis not the herdsman's cattle, but the Chief's cattle that he looks after."

"Then keep the money for Clanranald."

The Boatmen murmur in Gaelic. From their tone they are urging Donald to accept the Prince's offer.

Donald relents, takes the coins. "If it is your command over a chief's, then I'll do it."

The Boatmen eagerly get up to a man, and pick up their weapons. They depart to do their business.

Charles smiles at Ned. "Well, Ned, is it butter and cheese for you, or will you have beef?"

"I'm a man of simple tastes, your highness, but by the grace of god, I shall have what is provided."

"You are not fussy after all?"

Ned is stirring the pot. "Not I, master. If a Prince can eat beef, then I certainly can eat beef as well as him, if not better."

O'Sullivan and O'Neil laugh.

"And what of wine?" Charles produces a bottle.

"If God has provided it, then I must not offend God."

"And if it has been provided by the Devil?

"Then, to the Devil with me!"

Captain O'Neil snorts. "You are a rogue, Ned Burke."

"I am, your honour, and here I find myself in roguish company in my homeland."

"You are from the Long Island?"

"I am a North Uist man. Ten miles from here no more."

O'Sullivan mocks him. "What will you do if you survive our roguery?"

"I will return to the humble occupation of being at one end of a sedan chair."

O'Sullivan states loudly. "There's ambition for you, Charlie. Not kingship and glory... but to carry city folks for a penny or two."

"It is a noble ambition, Ned."

"Yes, master. I know my place."

"Indeed you do, Ned, and we are happy with it. He is a splendid fellow is he not, gentlemen?"

Captain O'Neil snorts again. "We have not tasted his cooking yet?"

They all laugh at Ned's expense.

With the tune of *Clan Ranald's Men* running through his mind, Charles watches the approach of fifty five year old Ranald MacDonald, chief of the MacDonald. With him are Neil MacDonald, the twenty-seven year old clan tutor, and three Clanranald Retainers.

Captain O'Neil and Colonel O'Sullivan stand either side of the Prince. It is plain to all that they are formidably armed and ready to give their lives for the Prince's safety.

"It didn't take him long to poke his nose in." O'Neil is openly hostile to the presence of Clanranald and his men.

O'Sullivan is more circumspect. "Your highness. We should treat Ranald MacDonald with caution. His sons came out for us, but the old fox has only his own interests at heart."

Charles steps forward to greet the MacDonald chief. "Clanranald! "

Clanranald kisses the Prince's hand. "Your highness. It is an honour to have you on Benbecula."

"It is an unexpected honour to be here. We were blown off course."

MacDonald eyes Charles's plaid suit. "My home is your home."

"Then escort us to your house, chief."

"I cannot do that, your highness. You would not be safe. May we speak privately?"

"Not without my staff."

Clanranald, Charles, O'Sullivan and O'Neil move out of earshot of the others.

"The Long Island Militia is looking for you."

"They think I'm on St. Kilda."

"Only an Englishman would fall for that nonsense, trust me."

"Can I trust you?"

"No one can be trusted. Thirty thousand pounds has been offered for your capture, dead or alive."

"Do you hear that, gentlemen? Thirty thousand pounds! My, my. I wouldn't even offer thirty pounds for myself, dead or alive."

There is weak laughter.

The Chief is not amused. "You are in mortal danger, sir. You are the most wanted man in the entire world.

"And you still have the favour of the Hanoverians?"

"My son Ranald does not. He got his head turned in Paris and followed you against my advice. My son Alistair too."

"They both have their own minds."

"They have both done great harm to my interests."

"And what interests are those, MacDonald?" O'Neil is ready for a fight.

"Who are these Irishmen? Mercenaries? Is this why you give the right flank to the Atholl Brigade instead of my sons?"

"General Murray ordered that."

"But you were in charge. And now it has all come to nought."

"A man can but try to change the world. Life is short."

"I have no desire to shorten my own life by having you on my land."

Neil MacDonald is talking with Donald MacLeod.

They break off and approach the Prince's party.

"Well?" Clanranald is impatient. "Will you play your part in this design, MacLeod?"

"Aye, I will."

"Are we to be informed of this design? Donald is my service."

Neil explains "And remains so, your highness. Donald has agreed to sail to Stornoway to charter a boat for you."

"I assume you can pay for it?" Clanranald asks roughly.

"I have funds, yes."

Clanranald nods to Neil to continue.

"For your part in this design, your ship was wrecked in Kintyre and you have landed here on your journey home."

"Where is home?"

"Orkney. You are Captain Sinclair, the Prince is your son."

"And what am I" O'Neil asks.

"You are the bo'sun, Graham."

O'Neil is not convinced by the plan. "Tis a far fetched scheme."

Charles stops O'Neil short. "Allow us a moment, please."

Charles, O'Sullivan and O'Neil huddle to discuss.

Colonel O'Sullivan is suspicious. "He could be making a trap for us."

The Prince is more willing to accept the plan. "I trust Donald MacLeod. If he is part of it, the plan is a true one. Felix?"

O'Neil shakes his head. "What options do we have? John?"

O'Sullivan surveys the surroundings. "None. This place is not defensible if the enemy finds us and attacks."

"Then we have to accept this wild scheme, gentlemen?"

O'Neil. "Yes."

O'Sullivan agrees with a nod of his head.

They rejoin the MacDonalds.

"We accept your plan."

Chief MacDonald half smiles. "It will take some days to arrange."

"I have one condition." O'Sullivan is an old hand at negotiation. "We want a comfortable house for the Prince while we wait?"

Clanranald is a man of influence. "I have a tenant with a large house on Scalpay."

Donald cannot help adding information to the conversation. "Donald Roy's sister. She married a Campbell."

Clanranald shoots Donald a look.

"I take it he is a Hanoverian?" O'Neil feels he is right to be wary.

"I am the laird. If I ask him to do it, he must accept."

The Prince makes a snap decision. "Then, we are in your hands, Clanranald."

"Get your boat ready, MacLeod."

"Aye, sir."

"Your highness, is this wise?"

"The decision is made, Felix."

Donald MacLeod moves sharply off.

Clanranald gives his parting shot. "Its a terrible wrong that has overtaken this land. When you are removed from it, I will sleep again." He kisses Charles's hand.

Neil and the Retainers are departing with Clanranald. Colonel O'Sullivan and Captain O'Neil follow him a little of the way to the edge of bog.

"You trust him?"

O'Neil does not take long to ponder O' Sullivan's the question. "No."

The boat with the Prince's party rows into a small loch. There is a fishing yawl pulled on to a sandy strip between protruding fingers of gnarled rock. Donald guides the boat in, brings it to rest in the shallows some yards from the yawl.

Donald leads the Prince, O'Sullivan, and O'Neil along the rocky shore of Scalpay.

Ahead there is a lonely rough-hewn house with a slate roof. About it is scattered the implements of a crofter and a fisherman.

A bearded man, in his mid-thirties, hurries from the house. He is carrying a musket. He comes straight towards them.

O'Neil raises his pistol to fire.

"Naw! That is your man Campbell!"

Donald leads the party forward, warmly greets Donald Campbell like an old friend.

Donald and his crew are transferring their belongings from their boat to the yawl. Campbell and his son Kenneth, a strong boy of fifteen, watch on.

"I'll take good care of her, Donald."

"Aye, you better, Donald. It was Cathy's father's wedding present to me."

"Och" says MacLeod "She's a fine boat like your woman, Donald."

"Aye, she's a devil to manage as well." He kisses his hand and slaps his hand on the keel. "Keep her into the wind, old man, sail a straight course and you'll be free of trouble."

Donald's men push the boat out into the shallows and get themselves aboard. Donald steers as Rory and the rest of the boatman settle in the boat.

The yawl's brown sail is raised and catches the breeze.

Campbell and his son watch them sail away.

Darkness has fallen. Inside the house there is a roaring fire in the big front room. Charles stands blocking it with his kilt lifted high to dry himself.

O'Sullivan raises an eyebrow. "Can you give us more heat, Charlie?"

"You're steaming like a kettle." O'Neil enjoys his own joke.

The Prince ignores their requests.

Catherine Campbell is the laying the table with the help of two of her children.

"I'm not offending you, Mrs. Campbell?

"Mister Sinclair???" Catherine is disturbed from her own thoughts.

"May I ask? How does a MacDonald marry a Campbell when there is such terrible history between your clans?"

Catherine is hesitant in her speech.

"Come, speak freely."

"The Campbell's are Whigs to the core. The only way to temper their badness is to breed it out of them."

The Prince laughs loudly.

"How many children do you have, Missus Campbell?"

"Five boys and seven girls."

The men take a quick in-breath of air.

"And they'll all be Campbells by their last name?" O'Neil says with a straight face.

"My children are MacDonalds. They may have a Campbell for a father, but they know who they are. Isn't that right, children."

The two children adore her. "Aye, mammy."

The scene touches the Prince but notices the creases put on Catherine by Scalpay life. "It cannot be an easy life farming this land."

"We manage well, sir. There are deer in our Harris forest. Tis eighteen miles in length. We have two thousand head."

"You are rich."

"We are tenant farmers, but Campbell uses the yawl for fishing. We don't do without."

O'Neil is up sniffing around the table. "Are you serving up venison or fish for us to sup on?" He waits in anticipation of her reply.

"Venison, sir, of course."

O'Neil grins in delight.

Charles claps his hands with joy. "Madam, you do not know what joy it is to escape the cooking of our servant Ned. He has been trying to poison us!

Catherine smiles politely as O'Sullivan roars with laughter.

A cow is stuck in a bog. Kenneth is trying to pull it out of the peat. Charles, out for walk, shouts down to him.

"Can I help you?"

"Aye."

Charles jumps down into the bog. "Where do you want me to push?"

"If you can just take Morag here...."

Charles puts his shoulder to the rear of the cow as Kenneth takes the tether at the cow's head and pulls.

The cow lurches forward. Charles falls into the mire.

Kenneth helps him up. "Are you well, Mr. Sinclair?"

"Never better." The Prince wipes the mire from his clothes that are now ruined. "What's your name?"

"Kenny."

"Campbell's eldest?" Charles gives up wiping himself. "This farm will be yours one day."

"I want to go to Nova Scotia."

"How so?"

"There's no great joy being a Campbell on the Long island."

"This is a fine piece of land."

"You think so?"

"Travelling, seeing the world, it is over rated."

"I've no been further than Stornoway."

"Then you don't know that only kings can dream of owning a forest of deer. You'd be a fool to give it up for a poor farmer's life in Nova Scotia."

Kenneth ponders the choice.

They coax the cow on to firmer ground.

"I think I've ruined this fine suit given to me by Borrodale's wife.

"Och. On Harris a man can have ten yards of tweed for a shilling."

"And the cost of a cow?"

"Thirty shillings."

Charles puts his arm around the boy's shoulders.

"Well, Kenny, we are richer by twenty nine shillings by saving your cow from the bog! I would call that a profitable day's work."

Charles is changing into a new philibeg (small kilt) and plaid.

O'Neil enters the room in haste. "There's a boatload of armed men coming in to land!"

Charles picks up his pistols, follows O'Neil out of the room.

Charles, O'Neil and O'Sullivan are lying in the heather priming their weapons.

On the shore, Campbell, cradling his musket, is faced with six armed men in MacKenzie kilts, led by a clergyman called MacAulay who has the face of a weasel. Kenneth stands just behind his father with a brace of pistols.

"Turn him over, Campbell!"

"And who might 'him' be?

"Don't take me for a fool. Turn him over! And his friends!"

"I will not. These men have my hospitality. By the old laws, they are under my protection."

"There is a thirty thousand pound reward, man!"

"Three or four thousand a piece is it? You will have to fight me for your blood money!"

Campbell raises his musket to his shoulder, takes aim at MacAulay.

"You are not for King George, Campbell!"

"I am for King Geordie and Hanover. But first and foremost I am a Highlander." He cocks his musket. "I am a dead shot, minister! Take no further steps on to my farm"

MacAulay's supporters visibly wither in courage. They lower their arms.

MacAulay looks back. "You MacKenzies. Shame is on you!"

"Hold your tongue for Sunday, MacAulay. All of you! Return to your homes and count your blessings."

"You'll be arrested for this. As God will have it, you'll hang Donald Campbell!"

MacAulay curses at his men as they turn and go back towards their boat. He follows them, haranguing them the whole way.

The Prince and his companions rise from the heather.

"Well done, Campbell. I couldn't have done it better myself with a dozen men." O'Sullivan clasps Campbell's hand.

The Prince is more restrained. "You had the chance to be a rich man, Donald?"

"I don't like clergymen telling me right from wrong. You are my guests. That is the end of the matter."

The Prince is concerned for Donald. "For thirty thousand pounds, Reverend MacAulay, he'll be back soon enough."

On that fact, they all agree.

Charles, O'Sullivan, O'Neil are packed for the road. Campbell, Catherine and her many children are assembled to see them off.

"Kenny will take you over the hills to Stornoway. Widow MacKenzie has a fine big empty house on the edge of the town.

O'Sullivan "Will we not frighten the life out of her?"

"There's a chance Mister O'Neil might." It is a moment of lightness. "She'll no let you down."

"I am in debt to you all."

Donald and his entire family bow and curtsey.

"Come, lets away before I cry." The Prince turns on his heel, steals a quick look backwards. The entire Campbell family are waving their farewells.

On the bleak shore of south Harris, the MacLeod boat lies abandoned.

The small party led by Kenneth enters the mist-hung oak forest. A gloomy damp evening descends on them as they weave between the ancient trees. Despite the lack of light, the trees gleam green with moss and the boughs are skinned by lichen. As they climb upwards, deer scurry and dart out of their way. The light is all but gone when the break through the tree line on to the green slopes.

They are now high in the hills. To the east is the faint outline of distant Skye. Below them to the south, there is a twinkle of a light from a shepherd's fire. To the north is black as the clouds roll over the hilltops towards them.

Ten minutes later, the weather turns wild and wet. The Prince trails his two companions who following Kenny along a narrow foot-wide track. It is not easy to see their way ahead. The rain is driving into their faces. Kenneth stops dead.

O'Sullivan bumps into him. "What's wrong, boy?"

"I cannae see a thing."

"What????"

"My eyes are nae good in the dark."

"How far do we have to go?"

"I cannae see. I'm lost."

O'Neil leans over O'Sullivan.

"Are you faking it, boy?"

"Naw, sir. I'd know where we are if there was light!"

"You are frightening him." The Prince pushes forward, gets between the boy and his companions. "Let's wait until the moon comes up."

O'Neil is mocking. "We'll be getting no moon tonight."

Charles takes Kenneth by the arm and finds shelter. They huddle against a rock. O'Neil and O'Sullivan find their own rock.

The rain drives down.

"Its a pretty pass we've come to, John."

"Reminds me of the weather in Kerry. You miss the old country, Felix?"

O'Neil wipes the rain from his face. "Aye, sometimes. I've been too long in France to go back."

"Fighting gets in your blood. It's the defeats I remember. We experienced some sore ones with Marshal Saxe. Especially Dettingen."

"Aye, but we got revenge on that jackanapes Cumberland at Fontenoy."

"For him to get us back again at Culloden?"

Both of them ponder the nature of their current defeat.

O'Sullivan gives a little smile. "When I was younger, this would have been adventure. Now, it just seems like bad planning."

O'Neil laughs at the irony. "A soldier's life is bad planning. We should have remained with Saxe instead of taking a commission with the Stuarts." He lowers his voice. "They are poor hands at fighting."

"Hush, Felix." O'Sullivan casts is eye to the Prince. He is pressed against the rock with Kenny. Both are shivering. O'Sullivan softens.

"How are you, young master?"

"Well enough, Colonel." The Prince disguises his misery.

O'Sullivan throws his eyes at O'Neil as if to say 'go easy'.

The two old soldiers, cold and wet, attempt to get some sleep.

It is a bright sunny morning. It is close to midday. There is little activity on the quay as the search for the Prince has disturbed the normal business of Stornoway town. A mob of around two hundred men has gathered at the quayside market. Reverend MacAulay is addressing them.

Kenneth is hiding behind a stack of netting. He cannot hear what MacAulay is saying, but he can tell from the reaction of the mob that he is stirring up trouble.

Old Donald, Ned and Neil MacDonald descend a gangway leading from the deck of a four hundred ton brig. Their departure is watched by the brig Captain and his Bo' sun.

Old Donald is livid. "He's gone back on his word. What sort of man says one thing then changes his mind five minutes later."

Ned is irritated. "You shouldn't have offered five hundred pounds to buy the ship. The moment you said it, he knew our cargo was the Prince."

Neil is determined his plan will succeed. "If they won't let us buy it, we'll steal it."

As they assemble on the quay, the MacLeod boatmen appear from hiding.

Rory is anxious for news. "Well, Donald? Have we the ship?"

"No, but Neil is for stealing it."

"Aye, we could. There are enough of us. How many on board?"

Neil addresses Rory. "I counted four. You think you could sail it to the mainland?"

"Aye. We could sail that hulk."

"Not without a pilot, Rory. We could wreck ourselves. Most of the boys have bairns." Donald looks to his own son.

"I'm for it, father."

The boatmen are talking amongst themselves.

Kenneth comes running. "Mister MacLeod!"

"What are you doing here, boy?"

"The Prince is in Stornoway."

"Could he no wait on Scalpay?"

Ned touches Donald on the shoulder and points.

The mob led by MacAulay is marching on to the quayside.

Neil takes Kenneth aside. "Hide yourself. If anything happens to us, you are to tell the Prince to go back to Benbecula. Understand?"

"Aye, sir." Neil waves Kenneth away.

As the mob draw closer, two of the MacLeod men run off in fear. The rest cock their muskets. Ned shuffles to the back to get behind them.

The Reverend MacAulay shouts." Donald MacLeod!"

Neil whispers in Donald's ear. "Show no fear, Donald, or we are done for." Neil cocks his own pistol.

Donald unarmed, steps forward.

The mob is within twenty feet of him.

"You have exposed us to great danger, MacLeod!"

"Away with your nonsense, man!"

"You brought Charles Edward Stuart HERE!"

"I did. Would you have had me take him to St. Kilda?"

The last of the mob has stopped shuffling. There is an intense expectation.

"I am not amused by your perfidy. As well as the Prince being on our island, he has an army of five hundred at his command!"

"Have you been drinking?" Donald gathers his voice so all can hear him. "The Prince has only two companions, and when I am there, I make the third!"

The mob takes this information in. MacAulay turns to face them. "I do not believe that Charles Edward Stuart has only two companions!"

"I told you it was three counting me." Donald raises his voice. "I tell ye, if your own Earl were here himself, by God he would not dare put a hand on the Prince!"

The mob breaks into open disagreement. Neil and the boatmen keep their weapons trained on the mob despite being overwhelmed by their enormous number.

An old man delivers some words into MacAulay's ear. The minister nods. "Put down your arms and we vouch that Stornoway will show no ill-will towards the Prince."

"Will you turn him over to Cumberland for the reward???"

There is a general hubbub. A few cries of "No" go up. A man shouts, "We do not want to be his executioners. Another "We just want him to leave the Long Island!"

"Then let us hire him a pilot, and we'll be gone!" Donald points to the brig.

There is more mumbling as the proposal is considered.

A cry goes up. "The fleet is back!"

The mob to a man rush to the edge of the quay and look seaward.

Sixteen warships are sailing in the Minch. They are no more than an hour from harbour.

"Captain Ferguson! God help you! We can do nothing for you now!" MacAulay is openly afraid of Hanoverian reprisals and the notorious naval commander in charge of the hunt.

"Let us pass!" Donald, Neil and the Boatmen brush past MacAulay and towards the mob. The men give way, and allow them free passage.

Kenneth runs after them. Clear of the quayside and sure that they are not being followed, they pick up pace and pass through the town led by Kenneth.

In widow MacKenzie's house, the Prince is getting a couple of hours sleep in an upstairs room. It is his first bed for many weeks and it is a deep sleep. Downstairs Mistress MacKenzie is fussing about in a tizzy. The presence of the Prince has made her most anxious about his safety. She cannot help herself, she is constantly at the window, fidgeting, wringing her hands in fear.

"The boy is back!" Mistress MacKenzie bounds from the window to the hall with such haste, O'Neil springs too with his pistol in his hand.

"Oh sit, Felix! I've had enough commotion for a lifetime!"

Donald and Ned enter the room carrying brandy, bread, and cheese. O'Sullivan and O'Neil perk up as they are handed the drink and food. Mistress MacKenzie kisses Kenny on the forehead, relieved that he is safe.

Captain O'Neil "Have we a ship, Donald?"

"The plan misgave. Neil says we are to sail back to Benbecula. He has gone on ahead by foot."

"To inform that old coot, Clanranald?"

Donald does not answer. He is old enough to know when to hold his counsel. Ned is not as long in the tooth. He is pleased to bend O'Sullivan's patience. "What a mob! Two hundred men at arms!"

"You are babbling, man."

Ned is suddenly perplexed. He looks about. "Where is the Prince?"

"He is out of sorts, Ned. We have had our fill of the Prince's moods."

There is the sound of movement from above.

O'Neil points upwards with his finger. "His highness stirs."

"And so he should! We are in immediate danger of being lynched!"

The Prince appears at the foot of the stairs.

"Lynched? Is this one of your tall tales, Ned?"

"No indeed, sir. No indeed!"

"Then bring me my supper."

The Prince, in off-hand manner, indicates to Ned to bring him some food and drink. He looks around the room and knows that things are not well. Donald is brooding.

"Why are you silent, Donald?" The Prince knows the news cannot be good. He loses his temper "Speak!"

Donald is lost for words "I'm an old man, your highness."

Ned takes the Prince his wants. He is conciliatory. "Donald was most bold with the mob, master."

"What mob?"

"Led by that minister from Scalpay! Donald made a him look a fool."

Donald is bashful. "I had taken a wee bit too much brandy with the captain."

Donald approaches the Prince and offers him a lit clay pipe, speaks softly. "I don't want to alarm you, your highness, but the frigates have returned from St. Kilda. We must leave the vicinity or we will be overtaken."

It is late evening and the light is fading. Young Donald is holding the painter of Campbell's yawl. The Boatmen, lingering on the stone jetty, are reluctant to get in the boat.

"Why are the men not ready?"

"They want to leave us, father."

Donald is unemotional. "I can't find fault with that given our cargo."

Charles overhears Donald. He addresses the boatmen.

"I beg for your service, gentlemen?"

The Boatmen look to one another.

"We must take to sea immediately. To wait longer will mean arrest and the hangman for all."

The men, surprised at being addressed by the Prince directly, turn to one another, converse in Gaelic.

"What are they saying, Donald?"

Donald seizes the moment. He addresses his men in their own tongue. "Do you want to be hanged, drawn and quartered?"

The boatmen shake their heads.

Donald singles out Rory. Again in Gaelic "Do you want to see the Prince beheaded and his fair head stuck on a spike as it surely will?"

Rory blanches at the thought of it. He turns to persuade the rest of the boatmen to get in the yawl.

Donald addresses the Prince. "The boat is at your service, your excellency."

The MacLeod boatmen are on board and prepared to sail. Old Donald is seating O'Sullivan and O'Neil. Ned is left to his own devices. The Prince is on the jetty pressing gold coins into the hand of Kenneth.

"We must away!" Donald shouts.

The Prince will not be rushed.

"Another cow for your mother, Kenny. And a yawl for your father, as I fear we will not be returning it."

Kenneth looks at the coins with wide eyes.

The prince gets into to the yawl. Young Donald casts off and steps into the boat as it pushes off.

Kenny watches in wonder as the Prince's party sail off into the night.

The men are rowing. The boat is hugging the Lewis shore.

O'Neil is confiding in O'Sullivan. "Any future Clanranald plan should be met with suspicion."

O'Sullivan whispers. "You think he designed to betray us."

O'Neil is devoid of tact. "He's a MacDonald!"

Two of the boatmen stop rowing, and stiffen. They glare at O'Neil.

Donald is quick to intercede. In Gaelic "Steady, boys. Captain O'Neil is an uneducated ignorant Irishman."

One of the boatmen curses, the other spits into the water.

O'Sullivan nudges O'Neil. "A couple of more MacDonalds."

Felix holds up his hands in apology. "Forgive me. I thought you were all MacLeods. Tis brave of you all to undertake our rescue."

The two boatmen accept the apology in a grudging way and start to row again.

It is morning. The yawl is making good progress. They are off the coast of Harris. The sail has been hoisted and most of the crew and the Prince's party are sleep, or trying to sleep.

Ned, crouched at the prow, is on lookout duty. Rory is at the helm.

Ned is fighting the cramp in his legs. He attempts to stand up, straightening one leg at a time. He manages to slowly uncoil himself and get vertical. He is unsteady on his feet, but manages to keep his balance. He takes a good look about, satisfying himself that he is a seaman at last, and that life on the ocean could be something to enjoy.

Suddenly, a glint of something catches his attention to the seaward. The yawl is bobbing up and down, but on the rises, there is no doubting what he is seeing.

"Frigates! A pair of them!!!" His shouting has the company in the boat startled. He continues to gesture seaward. In the near distance, two ships are plainly visible.

Donald and his son drop the sail. They gather it in as the boatmen take to the oars. The sea spray soon makes them fully awake. They have grasped the enormity of the danger. They quicken their strokes.

The Prince tries to stand to snatch a glance at the ships, but Rory has turned the yawl towards the shore, and the kick of the waves makes it impossible for the Prince to remain upright for more than a few seconds.

"Have they seen us?"

Donald with his vast experience, balances himself on a cross plank long enough to size the situation. The Prince grasps hold of Donald and steadies himself. "The light is on them but not us." Donald looks up. "As long as that cloud blocks the sun, we will be blind to them."

The Prince focuses on a large grey cloud that is playing peek-a-boo with the sun. A shaft of brilliant white light breaks through, floods the water a mere fifty yards from the stern of the boat. He watches in fear as the shaft of light moves towards them but dies just feet from their starboard.

They are in the hands of fate.

The sea turns dark and rain descends on the open boat. The shower turns into a lashing squall. The Prince and his companions are put to bailing. The boatmen continue to pull towards the shore with all their might.

The boat is beached off the coast of Lewis on a small island called Iubhard that in antiquity had a small fort on one of its two hillocks. The horizon is cloud laden. There is a fierce wind.

The Boatmen are onshore sheltering under the sail. Nearby there is an abandoned habitation. It is little more than a thatched hut with a roof shot with holes.

Inside, the Prince's party has been settled. It is a miserable abode in which a fire has been lit. The Prince is drunk on brandy punch. O'Neil is finding him insufferable.

"My friends would laugh to see me now. This place is like a hovel in a Versailles play." He is rambling. "Louis of France is a handsome fellow like me. A man of his word. But a king and his council are two very different things, two very different things!"

He turns to Ned who is cooking fish.

"Ned! I will recommend you to my father for a knighthood. Sir Edward Burke! I can't wait to tell him about my magnificent adventure!"

O'Sullivan and O'Neil have been drinking too, but they are not drunk. O'Neil has had his fill of the Prince. "Four days of this hovel, John. Mixed with the smell of Ned's cooking, I can't stomach any more."

O'Neil gets up, pushes past Donald, and out of the hut.

The Prince is oblivious. "More punch, Ned!"

"You've drunk it all, master."

"Make some more!"

"We have no brandy nor sugar left, master. I would make punch from fish but it would be a miracle as mighty as Jesus feeding the five thousand."

Charles, rebuffed, staggers out of the door.

Outside, O'Neil is taking a piss. Charles joins him in the buffeting wind.

O'Neil is sharp in his tone. "This is a God forsaken place."

"Its part of my father's kingdom..."

O'Neil let's out a dismissive hiss.

The Prince detects his derision. "He has been paying you to fight for him, not me."

"Aye, but why weren't you happy to have Scotland for the Stuarts and leave England alone?"

"I'm as much English as Scottish, Felix. My great grandfather Charles was born in England, my grandfather and own father too. My father is the rightful king of England, Scotland and Wales. Ireland too, remember that. I couldn't stop at Scotland.

"And now he has this as his only possession."

Charles, numbed by the brandy punch, is devoid of bitterness, or regret. "Its a nice little island. Short of amenities and provision, but a nice little island just the same.

"Tis a rock. And we have climbed under it. Louis has deserted you."

"No, not at all."

"Then where is our ship for France?"

"Its out there."

"Where exactly?"

Charles suddenly realises that O'Neil is challenging him. "Are you doubting me, Felix?

"I'm doubting Louis's resolve to rescue you."

"It will be done!" He is annoyed with O'Neil's lack of faith in him.

"Not if we stay in this wasteland!"

O'Neil turns angrily back towards the hut.

Inside the grim abode, O'Sullivan watches as O'Neil gathers his belongings. "I'm leaving. John? Are you with me?"

O'Sullivan does not need to be asked twice. "I am." He gathers his own scattered belongings stored in the broken walls. "Donald? Get your men prepared."

"Its dangerous, Colonel. The wind is close to gale. The men will not do it. Let's put it off to tomorrow?

"You've said that for the last three days. Go and speak with them! If they don't get in that boat tomorrow morning, I'm going to shoot them one by one until they do!"

The Prince is hanging by the door.

"Your highness." Donald sullenly leaves the hut.

There is silence. O'Sullivan standing with his possessions in his arms, puts them back in the walls.

"Is supper ready, Ned?"

"Aye, master, I think we all need some of Ned's fare to stop us from killing one another." He lifts the pot off the fire.

O'Neil utters a huffy noise, throws himself on the ground, and covers himself with a plaid. O'Sullivan, equally disinterested in Ned's cooking, backs into the shadows.

Ned is stumped by the apathy "Its fine herring you'll be getting here."

The Prince is hungry. "I'll gladly eat it!"

"You love my cooking, master."

"Love is a strong word, Ned."

The weather is fair and the Prince and his party are once more back at sea in the boat. They are bobbing on the waves and gazing towards a man o' war that has appeared on the horizon.

The Prince is sober and remorseful. His head is cradled in his hands as he comes to terms with his hangover. "Is it French???"

O'Neil stands up with a spyglass. He fixes a sight on the distant ship. "Its a sloop of war. The Furness! Ferguson's ship!"

Charles raises his head from his hands. "They will surely see us?"

Aboard the HMS Furness, Captain John Ferguson, an Aberdonian with a strong dislike for Highlanders, has a spyglass to his eye. "It is they! Give the order to pursue. Get Lieutenant MacCaghan up here!"

A naval officer carries out his order "Aye, sir!"

The ship unfurls its full sail – veers landward towards the fugitives.

Captain O'Neil still has his spyglass on the Furness. "She's turning this way!"

Donald is quick to respond. "Make haste for the shore, boys"

Lieutenant MacCaghan, a young army officer in his twenties, decked in the bright red uniform of the Royal Scots Fusiliers, joins Ferguson on the poop deck.

"There is our man, Lieutenant!"

MacCaghan takes the spyglass. "I think you are right, sir."

"Of course I am right, man! When we get into the shallows, I want you to put down a long boat with as many of your men as you can get in it!"

"Do you want him dead, sir?"

"Alive, you idiot! I may be friendly with Cumberland, but I will not get my thirty thousand pounds unless I deliver the Young Pretender to him in person."

O'Neil is monitoring the progress of the Furness. "She's come in as far as she dares. She's put down a long boat."

"Do we outnumber them?" O'Sullivan asks.

"They must have twenty to thirty Redcoats plus the crew."

The long boat commanded by MacCaghan is packed with Fusiliers each with a musket. Marines, armed with pistols and cutlasses, are rowing.

The Prince's boat is now close to the shore. Behind them, the long boat is gaining steadily.

The Boatman put all of their sinews into their rowing. The boat rounds a rocky point. Ahead lies a rocky bay with towering cliffs.

Donald MacLeod instructs his men. "Get under the cliffs!"

Rory steers the boat between two clefts of rock. As Charles looks down, he sees the rocky bottom through the clear waters.

"Heave to!" Donald is barely audible over the crash of the sea on the rocks. The Boatmen are fending off the cliffs with their oars. "Steady boys..."

Charles, O'Sullivan, O'Neil and Ned are in a state of heightened agitation. They are priming their weapons.

The long boat is heading towards the cliffs. The Marine Sergeant is looking ahead. "Shallow water! Rocks below!"

The Marines stop rowing.

"What's the matter, man?" MacCaghan is annoyed with the Sergeant for the pause in the pursuit.

"We are so heavily laden with your men, their draft is half of ours! In this swell we could get swamped!"

MacCaghan looks about. "Can you land us?"

"No, sir. We'll break our back on the rocks!"

Over the dim of the sea, the Prince's party can hear the shouting.

O'Neil strains to see the longboat by gripping on to the cliff and pulling the boat slightly into sight of the long boat.

A volley of shots flies past O'Neil's head.

He scrambles the boat back behind the cover of the rocks.

MacCaghan hurries to the prow of the longboat. Two Redcoats are reloading their muskets.

"Did you hit the target?"

"No, sir" a man replies.

MacCaghan strains to see the Prince's boat for himself but cannot.

The Sergeant is angry. "You are putting the men's lives at risk, sir! We will sink if we remain here!"

MacCaghan straightens. "Damn it! We have them! They have to come out at some point!"

"We are scraping the bottom, sir." MacCaghan looks over the side. "We'll have to turn about, sir. Captain Ferguson won't like it if we drown."

"He'll take it out on me, sergeant, if I don't return with the quarry!"

"You have a thick skin, sir. You'll be alright."

Some of the Redcoats are being sick.

MacCaghan waves his arm in frustration. "You have your way, sergeant!"

"Row out! Row out!" the Sergeant shouts

The Marines begin to back row pull out of danger.

O'Neil is strains forward again. "They're pushing off."

Donald takes a quick look. Smiles. Gaelic. "Ship your oars!"

The Boatman to a man lift their oars clean out of the water and lay them along the gunnels. They are exhausted.

The boat has moved out from under the cliff and is resting in a small cove. O'Neil is once more using his spyglass to monitor the enemy.

"The long boat has returned to HMS Furness."

"Have they given up?" asks the Prince.

"That is wishful thinking. Too many men in their boat." He looks again and sees the disarray with which the soldiers are climbing back aboard the ship. The ship's marines could sit out in the open water all day long, but not with soldiers with them."

"Soldiers detest the sea," O'Sullivan adds. He is talking about himself.

"Well, the enemy know where we are now." The Prince is resigned to the situation.

"Catching us is another matter," Donald adds. "I'm no a master sailor for nothing." He pats his son on the shoulder. "We'll wait here till dark and give them the slip."

It is dark. There is a partial moon. The men are rowing.

Donald is looking out to sea. "I don't see the ship's lights."

The others look.

"I think we've put a fair three leagues between ourselves and the Redcoats. Ship your oars, boys."

The boatmen do as they are told as Donald drops an anchor. "Its two hours to the sun comes up. Get some sleep."

As the boat bobs in the sea, they rest as best they can.

The Prince is cold, hungry and restless. He is in a miserable state of depression at his own misfortune. "Where are we, Donald?"

"That dark line over there is Ronay. We're not far from Benbecula." Donald is concerned for the Prince's health. "Are you fine, your highness?"

The Prince hides his true feelings. "I am, Donald, just fine. And your lad there?"

Young Donald is asleep, his head resting on Donald's lap. "He's a fine boy, on a fine adventure. I was just a bairn at his age."

"He's a fine young man. Where's his mother?"

"Och, Catherine, she's waiting for us in Skye. I said I would be back ten days ago. She'll be thinking I'm with some other MacDonald woman."

They share a laugh. There is little else to share until the dawn.

The low-lying eastern coastline of Benbecula with its maze of little bays is a rocky wasteland of narrow inlets and hidden bays.

The boat rows through a narrow channel into Uskavagh Bay.

They pull on to the shingle on one of the many small islands peppered throughout the loch. A strong gale is starting up.

The Prince looks up at the sky.

The party takes shelter in a bothy.

It is three days later and it is a more miserable place than Iubhard.

The wind is wild and unhindered in its ferocity as it blows from the west across the low-lying bog land that composes most of Benbecula. Time has not changed the island much since the thaw of the Ice Age.

The hut's entry is very narrow. They have to creep in on their bellies to enter it. Inside, two Boatmen are plucking sea birds for supper. The rest are mending fishing net with the plan to cast it in the loch for herring.

The Prince wriggles out of the hut. His clothes are a sorry state from his late travails. He has also sprouted a beard, and as is the custom of his forefathers, it is red in colour. In all respects he is Stuart, his line of kings going back to Robert the Second, the grandson of the Bruce.

As Charles looks out across a stretch of water to the Benbecula mainland, he sees Donald and Young Donald approach across the bog-sodden moor with Neil MacDonald.

The Prince waves to them. They wave in return.

He watches as they cross the sands that are covered with water when the tide is in. He greets them on the beach.

"Donald! Send me to some Christian place! This hut is a monstrous hole!"

"Your highness. We are to go with Neil to a better abode."

The Prince looks at Neil. "Your last scheme failed, MacDonald?"

Neil is apologetic. "Forgive me. I follow my chief's instructions. I am only the Clanranald family tutor. However, my brother Ranald has a house in South Uist ... in a glen called Corrodale."

And so to Corrodale. Less than a quarter day from Benbecula, the Prince's party sail their boat to a shingled little cove.

The tired men file from the beach and ascended a heather covered bank. Before them, stretches a glacial valley covered in green pasture. In a small clump of trees stands a modest abode.

"That is the forester's house. My grandfather had it from the old Clanranald chief before they fell out."

"Where's the forest?"

"Long gone for charcoal before my grandfather's time. As you see, the trees that remain part conceal the house from the sea."

The house is little more than a summer retreat that appears to have been neglected for some time. Charles is standing in front of the house looking out. He has a comprehensive view of the glen and bay, but the trees obscure much of the open sea and the view to the rude mountains of Rum.

"It is safe here?"

"As safe as you can be with three thousand men looking for you."

"That many?"

"Thirty thousand pounds is enough incentive for any man. Come, I will show you the interior."

A little more than a humble summer cottage, the house is now in a better state of repair. The Prince emerges from its interior in healthy spirits followed by O'Sullivan.

There is the sound of digging.

"What are they doing, John?"

"Felix has instructed the men to dig an escape chamber."

"Escape to where?"

O'Sullivan leads the Prince some twenty yards

around a spur to the back of the cottage. O'Neil is stripped to the waste and digging like blazes.

"The tunnel will come out here behind this boulder. The ground is quite soft. They are making great progress."

"Is this necessary?"

"Its a precaution, Charlie."

Charles flops down on to a boulder.

"I have failed my father and the Stuart cause. I still don't understand why at Derby the council overrode me and turned the army for home."

"Fear. It was fear. You had done something that the Spanish and French have only dreamed of."

"What is that?"

"Invade England."

"But why did the people not come out for me? We barely got fifteen hundred recruits and all of those from Manchester."

"Catholics are more hated in England than German King Geordie." O'Sullivan is a Catholic like the Prince, like most of his followers. "Then there's the Parliament. We would never have got the Whigs on our side, but we would have had Tories if the plan had been carried through."

"Murray of Broughton was in charge of that."

"Another Murray. You were badly advised by him. Deserted us too after Derby."

"Do you think he sensed the cause was lost?"

"I'm a soldier. I live for the next battle. I don't get paid to think ... thinking is the province of princes."

"It all comes down to money, not loyalty."

"Normally an army lives on the generosity of Princes. Your Highland army survives on loyalty. If you stay loyal to them, they will not desert you."

"Yet, they have."

"No, they have not. You have given up the fight and sent them home."

"Perhaps that was a foolish thing to do..."

"My design has always been to fight on. Now, here we are, reduced in numbers, and the larder is bare." O'Sullivan picks up a musket, hands it to the Prince. "Charlie. You are still the best marksman amongst us. Felix and I would like some supper other than fish."

The Prince smiles at the old soldier, takes the musket.

The Prince is hunting with Burke. He raises his musket – fires.

He brings down a deer.

"Well done, master!" shouts Ned. Burke immediate starts running towards the carcass. While the Prince re-primes his musket, Ned reaches the dead animal, drops down on his knees, and begins draining the blood.

Then as if from nowhere, a small island boy, about ten years old, dressed in rags, appears at Burke's side.

Ned looks up at him in surprise.

"Where did you come from?"

The boy doesn't answer, stares at Ned as if he is an alien creature.

Ned stands up and turns to shout to the Prince. "Master!"

The Prince looks up from his task at hand. "Yes, Ned?"

Ned turns and points.

The boy is on his knees cutting a hunk of meat from the hind of the deer.

"You little thief!"

The boy takes his slice of meat, and flees.

Ned gives chase and in no time catches the boy. He takes hold of him, snatches the meat from him, and raises the back of his hand to strike him.

"No, Ned!" Charles grabs Ned by the wrist. "Tis a child!"

"He's a little thief, master!"

"Ned! I'll not see a Christian child want for food and clothes whilst I can help it."

The boy stares open mouthed at the Prince.

Charles places his hand on the boy's shoulder. "Don't be afraid, lad."

He shrugs the Prince's hand off.

"He doesn't understand English."

"You speak Erse, Ned. Talk with him. Where did he come from? Ask him that?"

In Gaelic "Where are you from, you wretch?"

"Boisdale."

The boy points to a high cliff above them. "I came down that way?"

"Why are you here? This land is private."

The boy is frightened. "I come here to collect eggs." He shows Ned a basket with bird eggs.

Ned, satisfied that the boy is not a spy, lets go of him.

Charles picks up the dropped venison, hands it to the boy.

The boy looks at Charles in awe, and backs off. He turns and runs off as fast his legs will carry him.

"He's off to inform on us like a Judas!"

"Nonsense, Ned."

"You are too lenient by far, master."

Ned kneels down to lift the deer on to his shoulder.

Charles glances up at the cliff.

Charles and Ned are standing on a narrow path that leads around the cliffs. A formidable mountain looms over them.

"So this is how the boy got into the valley?"

"Aye, its only wide enough for one man at a time. Will you put a guard on it, master?

"To what end? If they come for me, Ned, there will be hundreds of them."

"Three hundred Greeks defended Marathon against a million Persians."

"With swords and shields." Charles points out to sea. "Nowadays, a few rounds from a ship's canon would put a stop to that in ten minutes.

The cottage is now in a fine state of repair. It is obvious that some days have passed and that the fugitives have settled in. The Prince is sitting on a stone that is before the door of the house with his face turned towards the sun. He is smoking from a frail, broken clay pipe given to him by Donald who is sitting a few feet away. Ned watches.

"Master, you will get yourself a headache."

"Get about your business, Ned! The sun is doing me all the good in the world."

Donald smiles, puffs on his own broken pipe.

The Prince removes his pipe from his mouth. "This is a bother, Donald!"

"It is, your excellency. Its a lot of puffing we have to be doing."

Charles picks up a knife and begins to trim a seagull feather. He cuts the feathers from the quill and puts it in the end of his pipe. He sucks on the new contraption.

"My, Donald, its the coolest smoke I'm having now." With the pipe clenched in his teeth, he takes Donald's pipe, puts another cut quill in the end of his.

"There my old friend!" He is most pleased with himself.

Donald sucks on his pipe, breaks into a smile.

"Are we not the finest men on the Long Island?"

"There's no doubting it, your excellency."

Charles begins to hum a highland reel. He rises smartly and starts to move his feet to his own humming. "Do you dance, Donald?"

"Not now. My knees have been got to by the sea."

Charles shows off his ability to dance, his two-step, his *pas de bas*, and his twirl, whistling along to 'The Mighty General Gathering' as he does so.

Donald puffs on his pipe contentedly, amused to be entertained by the Prince.

A small boat is pulling into the bay. Neil joins the Prince and Donald in front of the house.

"Who is that, Neil?"

"Its Clanranald himself paying a visit."

"He is very hot and cold with me."

"He's not a great papist, your excellency."

"Nor am I. I never agree well with priests. However, I make my prayers to God every morning and that suffices. Come; let's welcome your kinsman. We still have much to thank him for."

The Prince waits on the grassy bank to greet the disembarking Chief accompanied by MacDonald Retainers carrying muskets and ammunition boxes. To the Prince's surprise, Captain MacLeod is leading the party carrying an armload of muskets.

"Alex! It is a warm sight to see you safe on Uist."

"Your highness! It is a relief to see you safe too!" They help to relieve him of the muskets.

The Retainers not carrying muskets, deposit clean shirts, some stockings, wine and brandy. Ned immediately inspects the bundle.

Chief MacDonald is out of breath from walking up the slope. The Prince offers his hand. Clanranald's lips barely touch his knuckles.

"You are well looked after here by Neil, your highness?"

"It is a Prince's palace, dear friend."

"Lady Clanranald has sent this suit for you. She stitched it herself with the help on my niece Flora."

Ned holds up a fine tartan suit. The Prince takes it from him. He gushes with gratitude.

"Most delightful! Truly delightful!" He is in a happy mood. "I only need the itch to be a complete Highlander!" He laughs at his own joke.

Clanranald is dour and emotionless. "I brought you the latest newspaper from London. I'm afraid it is a week old. You are reported on almost every page."

Charles takes the paper. "I will read every line. There is little to do here but take the air and climb the hills."

Captain MacLeod is standing with an anxious look. The Prince takes heed that there are important matters to discuss.

"Come up to Corrodale Palace so I can offer you my hospitality."

Inside the house, Charles is seated on a turf throne softened with moss. He is glancing at the newspaper. He does not like what he is reading about himself.

Ned is seating MacDonald and Captain MacLeod. O'Sullivan and O'Neil hang back at the doorway while Donald lurks in a corner. Neil is likewise in the shadows.

Alex MacLeod is quick to divest his news. "Two French ships arrived off Arisaig four days ago. But it went badly. They were attacked by three British sloops and were engaged in a twelve hour gun battle."

"Were they sunk?"

"Fortunate, no, sir. The British ships ran out of shot and broke off for repairs. Our ships made haste inshore and off loaded our supplies with Secretary Murray."

O'Sullivan is quick to cut in. "Why did they entrust the cargo to him?"

"He is the most senior figure left on the mainland and the French would not entertain me. I showed them your order, but they would not accept an order written in English."

"For goodness sake! I love the French but they take their bureaucracy to the limit!"

The Prince is eager to know more. "What cargo did they give Murray?"

"Six hundred muskets, thirty thousand ball, military stores. And forty thousand louis d'or."

"That's eighty thousand pounds!" O'Sullivan is in a temper. "They've given that rogue enough money to pay two thousand men for a year!"

"Some young MacDonalds led by Ranald made off with one of the casks of coin. I got left a dozen of the muskets."

Clanranald is equally angered. "I resent the inference that members of my family have stolen from the Prince."

"Then what can we infer? That Murray has taken most of the money and that the MacDonalds have taken what's left???"

"Gentlemen!" The Prince rises. "This will not do! Calm yourselves!"

O'Sullivan and MacDonald cool their tempers.

"Were any of my other officers there, Alex?"

"Yes, sir, but Doctor Cameron took charge. He asked Secretary Murray to hand the money over to Cluny MacPherson for safekeeping. He refused."

O'Sullivan is livid again. "MacPherson is another rogue! They are all rogues!"

"John. Please restrain yourself. I must have calm if I am to issue my orders."

O'Sullivan nods. Meanwhile, O'Neil is kicking his heels together. His anger is rising.

"Donald. Prepare your men to take Captain MacLeod back to the mainland."

"Aye, your excellency." Donald scurries off.

"What's reason for me to return to the mainland, your highness? The French have sailed. They took Colonel Elcho, Sir Thomas and many others with them." MacLeod eyes O'Sullivan and O'Neil.

"I want you to find Doctor Cameron. You are to go with him and get Secretary Murray to return all of the gold. I will give you my order in writing."

"If Murray refuses?"

"He is a coward. Threaten him with hanging, and he will comply."

"Aye, your highness."

"Ned, get me paper and pen!"

Ned rises, goes into another room.

"Clanranald. I must request that you enquire into the conduct of your young MacDonalds."

Ned reappears with a small portmanteau.

"As you wish, your highness. It is a pity you are to remain here in discomfort. If you had remained in Moidart, you would now be on your way to France.

"I thank you for your observation."

Charles signs the paper, hands it to MacLeod.

"Make haste, Alex. Murray may attempt to flee for the continent."

"Your highness!" MacLeod departs.

The Prince picks up his pipe, begins to put tobacco in the bowl.

Clanranald rises. "I will leave you to your tobacco."

"You don't like me do you, chief?

"My sons have supported you against my will. My family's wealth is squandered and now I must depend upon the income of my wife. A man is judged by his position, not his temperament."

"And how see you my position?"

"I see it plainly. A child is ridiculed for saying that men are hiding in a glen. He is told that he deserves to be thrown into the sea for his pernicious nonsense. Yet, everyone knows about the men hiding in the glen. It is an open secret."

The Prince throws it back at the chief. "For how much longer?"

"Until you decide to leave the Long Island." Clanranald bows obsequiously.

The Prince half-heartedly offers his hand. Clanranald waves it away in a manner that suggests he is done with playing second best to the young Prince.

"Good day." He shuffles past the two Irish officers. They each give him a look of contempt as he exits to join his waiting retainers.

O'Sullivan throws himself on to a stool. "I swear that old coot is playing with us."

"Well, whatever game he is playing, he has not turned me in for the thirty thousand. What do you think, Felix?"

O'Neil turns and looks out the door at the departing MacDonalds. "I think we should get out of this place before the Redcoats come swarming over the hills."

Neil steps out of the shadows. "We will give you plenty of warning of that. You will be send word if there is any danger."

O'Neil is not convinced. "But if it's an open secret that we are here, then the enemy must know too."

Neil is matter of fact. "You do not know the people of the Uists. Of all the places in Scotland to keep a secret, it is the Uists. Rest here safely, your highness, the whole island is keeping watch over you. You will be informed when it is time to leave."

"You are a dark horse, Mister MacDonald."

"I am, sir, and so I must remain. I will return with Clanranald to Benbecula and collect intelligence of the enemy's movements. Be ready to leave within five minutes when the word finally comes. Adieu, your highness. Gentlemen."

Neil MacDonald leaves swiftly.

"What do you make of him, John?" O'Neil asks. "I can't make head or tail of that man."

"He is a mystery, I admit. He is by far the best educated of the entire MacDonald clan."

"Yet, we know nothing of him. What is your view, Charlie?"

The Prince is watching Neil race down the hill to catch up with Clanranald. "I would say that man is the brains behind our good fortune not to have been taken a month ago. I believe he is briefing Clanranald to remain neutral in our cause as it is the best course of action for our safety."

O'Neil and O'Sullivan are baffled by the Prince's deduction.

The Prince and Ned are out stalking for the day's kitchen. Ned is laden with four muskets. The Prince is wearing the MacDonald plaid suit made by the Clanranald women.

"I have become accustomed to sporting the MacDonald colours."

"I prefer the Stuart tartan myself. Its the red in it from all the blood ..." Ned checks himself.

"Come now, Ned, you know me well enough to be forthright. Speak freely."

"Well, I ken that all the red is from the blood of kingship, your honour. Four hundred years is a mighty long time for one family to lord it over everybody else."

"I agree, dear friend, but kingship is a burden, not a privilege."

"You think so? I wouldnae call lording it yon big houses and castles was a burden on anyone else but the servants keeping them clean."

"Yes, perhaps you have something there."

They are now out on the wild hillside high above the Corrodale valley floor. The Prince gets Ned to crouch with him in the heather. Feeding pheasants densely inhabit the hillside.

While Ned lays out the muskets for quick handing to his master, Charles is educating Ned on the ways of hunting.

"My great great grandfather."

"What king was that, master?"

"James the Sixth, First of England. He banned peasant shooting with firearms."

"How were they caught then?"

"Three methods - netting, liming and trapping."

Ned hands the Prince one of the firearms. He takes aim

Ned hands him the remaining three muskets in succession. He shoots down a bird each time.

They get up and start the process of finding the shot birds lying in the thick bracken.

"I am melancholic, Ned."

"And I, master. Look at my foot."

Ned lifts his right foot to reveal it has no shoe.

The Prince holds up his own feet one by one to show that his shoes have no soles.

"What have we come to, master?"

"Indeed, Ned. All my foolish confidence in Louis of France, that he will rescue me. It has come to nought."

Ned finds one of the downed birds. "Tonight I'm going to pray to God to help us."

"Things must be bad Ned if you are praying for us."

"Aye, everybody is doing it, but it's no working. Maybe if old Ned here puts in a good word He'll take pity on us."

They both laugh. The Prince takes a piece of leather from a pouch.

"Tis a sorry tale. The Prince and his Cinderella. But here, wrap this around your pretty foot as a slipper. I will have no servant of mine barefooted."

Ned raises the pitch of his voice to sound like a girl "Your highness is so kind."

"Seriously though, Ned. I doubt we will ever get away from this valley."

"Titch, titch, master. That will be in my prayers tonight."

"I'm glad of it."

Ned finds another bird.

"Master? Does a man close his eyes when he prays?

"Only when he is not on the run."

It is the fifth of June, and a platoon of Redcoats of Guise's 6th Regiment of Foot is lined up on the south Barra beach. Captain Caroline Scott, a favourite of Prince William and whose godmother is his mother Queen Caroline, is haranguing them.

"This island is called Barra. It is the southern tip of what the savages here call the Long Island. In fact, it is a string of islands and we are going to work our way up them until we find our quarry. We have been sent to this waste place to do our duty!"

"We saw the heathens off at Fort William. We slaughtered them at Culloden! We have burnt their foxholes in Appin! Now our orders are to find this Young Pretender? You are to show the wretches of these islands no mercy. You may take the women, you may hang the men, and you may slaughter their cattle! You may smash their ploughs, burn their crops, burn their hovels, and steal every possession worth taking!"

There is a cackle of laughter. A soldier whispers to his left "He doesn't like this lot, does' 'e?"

"Godson of the Queen, an all."

Scott lets the laughter subside. "This is no laughing matter. This Young Pretender has caused our majesty King George and the people of our nation a year of sleepless nights. We are here to put an end to that!"

Caroline turns to his Sergeant Quartermaster. "Quartermaster! Every man is to have twenty rounds! The first man to expend his rounds will have a guinea! God save the King!"

All return "God save the King!"

Donald, Young Donald and Captain MacLeod have returned from the mainland and are moving in haste from the shingle shore, up the slope towards the Corrodale house. O'Neil greets them.

"Neil MacDonald has informed us that the entire regiment of the 6th Foot have been put ashore on Barra." MacLeod has urgency about him. "Three hundred MacLeods of Skye militia have been landed on Benbecula."

He gestures by slowly bringing his hands together. "They are going to sweep from north and south. There will be no escape.

O'Neil is quick on the uptake. "Follow me!"

Donald gestures Young Donald to stay put. He follows the other two towards the cottage.

Ned is in a frenzy gathering possessions - clothes, arms, food.

The Prince is dressing for the imminent journey.

"Did you find Secretary Murray?"

"Aye, we did. Doctor Cameron got some twelve thousand louis d'or out of him."

"And the rest?"

"He did not answer other than to say that he had no other monies in his possession."

"Do you have the gold with you?"

"No, sir. It was in two large casks that would have sunk the boat. We hid them in a wood near Lochiel's house."

O'Sullivan is surprised. "The house is still intact?"

"It was when we arrived. We had to flee when a party of Redcoats led by Major Lockhart arrived. They set fire to it and burned it to the ground.

"Are these the facts, Donald?"

"Aye, your excellency. The young Captain, the Doctor and myself had a narrow escape."

"And Murray?

"Secretary Murray made off to the Lowlands."

O'Sullivan is sanguine. "The swine. Where's Doctor Cameron now?"

"He's gone to find Lochiel. He believes he is sheltering with Cluny MacPherson."

O'Neil is incredulous. "I find it hard to believe that in six weeks he hasn't been able to find his own brother. There's scheming going on...."

Charles cuts O'Neil short. "You have served me well, gentlemen."

O'Neil won't let it go. "You are both MacLeods?"

Alexander and Donald exchange glances.

Donald speaks up. "Aye we are, sir."

"Three hundred MacLeod militia are on Benbecula are helping the Redcoats to look for the Prince?"

"Aye, sir, that is correct."

"That's a lot of MacLeods. How do we know you are not aiding the Redcoats?"

Donald MacLeod smiles sweetly. "You know us not, Captain. We are MacLeods, that is true, but not from Skye. Fraternity we know, but we enjoy our own liberty and our own individual worth. The Prince has our loyalty, and the offer of a fortune will not dislodge us from it. Unlike yourself, we are not soldiers of fortune, we are simple men, with simple notions of what is right and wrong."

The Prince breaks in with a joyous outburst.

"Well said, Donald! Well said! There you have it, Felix. These men are idealists. That's what carried us to Derby! Belief in right and wrong. Well done, well done!"

The Prince offers some tobacco to Donald. He accepts. Together they start down the hill towards the boat.

O'Sullivan slaps Captain MacLeod on the shoulder, jokes. "How would you like to be my number two?"

O'Neil walks off in disgust.

"Don't judge Captain O'Neil. He is a good soldier. He has a strong nose for survival. That's the game now, lad, survival."

Ned exits from the cottage loaded with possessions. "Are they not in the boat yet! Heaven help us!"

Ned starts down the hill towards the shingled shore.

O'Sullivan is amused. "Where did you find him, Alex?"

"When I was studying law in Edinburgh, he carried me one drunken night in a sedan from the University to Muiravonside. He never left."

O'Sullivan laughs.

They follow the others down the hill.

The weather is foul. Wind and rain. The Prince's party is huddled in the boat as it heaves in the waves.

Donald, Young Donald and his Boatmen fight with the sea.

A day has passed. The weather is still atrocious. The boat is tied up on a rocky shore. The Prince's party shelter in a cleft of rock as the gale continues.

A boy in MacDonald colours, his plaid flapping wildly, is looking down on them. He is signalling frantically.

Young Donald scrambles up to him. The Prince watches as the two boys talk.

"This weather shelters us from our enemies."

O'Sullivan, sheltering next to the Prince, appears to be in pain.

"Are you well, John?

"I hurt my leg on the rocks getting out of the boat."

O'Sullivan's leg is badly mangled.

Young Donald returns and speaks with his father. Old Donald approaches the Prince. "That was Boisdale's boy. The militia are two miles away. They are sheltering in a shieling."

The party resign themselves to another night on the rocks.

There is a mist hanging on the water. The Boatmen are rowing quietly. Everyone is listening for the smallest noise.

O'Neil, armed and ready, is with Rory at the prow. He is staring intently ahead. Rory raises his arm.

Donald "Ship the oars."

The boatmen pull in their oars.

Distant VOICES.

O'Neil strains to make them out. "English..."

They listen. There are further muffled sounds.

Rory spots an object looming out of the mist.

The object comes into view. It's a rock....

The boat glides slowly past the rock.

The mist suddenly thins. The mast of ship is seen.

O'Neil "The Furness..."

The Boatmen quickly push their oars back into the water, stop the boat dead.

They listen. There is the sound of splashing oars and multiple voices.

O'Neil "English marines.... coming back from shore."

The VOICES are growing louder.

"Turn about...." O'Neil has his pistol levelled into the mist.

The Boatmen spin the boat, in quick order turn about.

Quietly they row back into the thicker mist.

The Prince's party are disembarking on an island to the left of the entrance to the loch. They are climbing on to the rocky outcrop of Calvey Island to shelter in the low walled ruin of the ancient castle. Like many of the islands of the Hebrides, they are connected to the mainland at low tide, and thus easy to reach on foot.

Thus perched on a bleak spot within sight of the harbour of Lochboisdale, if it were not for the height of the castle ruins, they would surely be discovered from the decks of the navy ships anchored all around the bay. For now the mist has blown off, and they are hidden from sight by the dark of the night.

The Prince, O'Sullivan and O'Neil are huddled around a fire burning dimly. Ned emerges into the faint light carrying a bundle of grass.

"For you, master."

"Ned, everyone is in need of bedding."

"Those islanders can pull their own mattress."

Captain MacLeod comes to the fire with Neil MacDonald.

The Prince is delighted to see Neil. "You appear everywhere, Mister MacDonald. I don't know how you manage to move so freely."

"It is not a skill, your highness. I know every track and way on the Long Island." Neil starts to unwrap a bundle.

"Do you have meat?" The Prince is ravenous.

"Butter and cheese. Some bread. Brandy. All from Boisdale's house."

"Let me have one of those bottles and a cut of bread."

Neil does as he is instructed. The Prince shares the food with his companions.

"There are fifteen sails in the bay."

O'Neil. "That's enough to conduct a foreign war."

O'Sullivan "Or end one."

Charles swigs on the brandy. "A fine feast. By account I have many well wishers in Lochboisdale."

MacLeod is quick to reply. "Hundreds, your highness. Lady Clanranald is the main architect."

O'Neil is shocked. "The old coot's wife???"

"My aunt Margaret is a MacLeod. My father's sister."

O'Neil" Well, I'll be damned. All this time and you never let slip that Clanranald's your uncle?

Neil clarifies the issue for O' Neil. "There's a score or more of MacDonald and MacLeod officers in the Militia. They've been passing information to Lady Clanranald about the Redcoats. That's how Alex and I get our information."

"Are the enemy close by?"

"Captain Scott's camp is a mile that way on the Lochboisdale road. He's in charge of the enemy cordon. Lochiel captured him at Highbridge."

"That Scott?"

"Aye, he was the first officer we captured in the campaign. We paroled him as he was wounded in the shoulder. When he was fit again, he took charge of the 6th Foot and was with Cumberland's men at Derby. He has no love of you, sir. He openly bragged to Cumberland that he would blast your head off if he encountered you. He was the enemy officer in charge at Fort William when Keppoch's siege failed. It's reported that it was Scott who shot Borrodale's son as he lay wounded at Culloden."

Captain O'Neil is incensed. "He's camped a mile from here you say?"

"Aye." MacLeod is stirring his own desire for revenge. "Scott is fresh from Barra. He hanged a man without trial two days ago."

Charles winces.

"Then let's go and put a bullet through his brain."

"No, Felix." The Prince is adamant.

MacLeod continues. "He had the skin flayed off the cattle there ... made them run mad about the island until they bled to death."

O'Neil springs up. "What sort of man is that? Lead me to him, MacLeod!"

The Prince rises.

"No. We will not be provoked. It is designed to make us reveal ourselves."

"He's a filthy Hanoverian!" O'Neil is incensed beyond reason.

"And a Scotsman. Sit down!" The Prince is angry.

O'Sullivan is more detached from the proceedings. "That's an order, Captain."

O'Neil reluctantly sits down. Neil hands him the brandy bottle.

MacLeod gives a low short whistle. The Boatmen appear carrying the sail of the boat.

They spread it out, and then with the oars they make a tent by pushing the sail upwards. They weigh the edges of the sail with rocks.

The rain has returned and is now beating down. All of the party, weary from two days of clinging to the rocks, take shelter in the makeshift tent.

The rain is drumming down on the windows of Boisdale House. The Redcoats have broken into the house and are roughly handing MacDonald of Boisdale and his son, the messenger boy to the Prince's party.

Captain Scott enters, sees Boisdale, and strikes him across the face. "We know you have been sending messages to him, Boisdale!"

Boisdale says nothing. Scott looks to the boy. He takes him by the left ear and twists it violently.

"What do you know, boy?" Boisdale's boy whelps in pain. "Well!"

The boy remains silent.

"You are foolish people! Sergeant! Take them out and give them a lashing."

Boisdale and his Boy are dragged out.

Lady Boisdale and her daughter are dragged in. They are tied neck to heel, and thrown to the floor.

"When will you MacDonalds learn not to help the enemies of the state? Strip them!"

Lady Boisdale cries out "No!"

Scott turns to his Quartermaster. "Bring them to me when you are done."

Scott leaves the women to the mercy of his men.

Neil MacDonald is running over the narrow stretch of wet rocks and sand that separate Calvey from the main island. Alex MacLeod closely follows him. They join with the Prince's party huddled under the sail.

"You must return to the mainland, your highness."

"I'm for it if it can be done in this weather?"

Donald is not optimistic. "There's a terrible swell."

MacLeod "We'd rather the Prince drowns than fall into the hands of the enemy. They are sparing no one."

There is the sound of splintering.

Donald is trying to work out what the sound is. It dawns on him. "My god! The boat!" He runs the short distance to the shore.

The boat is sinking. The MacLeod boatmen are scurrying across the rocks with the intention of wading to the main island. Young Donald and Rory are standing in a stupefied state.

Donald cries in Gaelic. "What was done to Campbell's boat?"

"The men have sunk her, Donald." Rory points, "They've run away in fear of being caught and tortured."

Donald is stricken with defeat. "We will all be caught now!"

"No, father!" Young Donald is unbroken. "We must save the Prince."

"Aye, son, you're right."

It is evening and the light is fading. The reduced party of the Prince, O'Sullivan, O'Neil, Ned, Donald, Young Donald and Rory are packed and ready to move when the order is given. O'Sullivan is perched on the Prince's luggage with his damaged leg. Charles is eating some mutton. Neil is keeping watch over the old battlements.

Captain MacLeod comes running across the narrow stretch of exposed sands. He jumps over a wall and advances to the waiting party.

"We are discovered! They have caught some of the boatmen."

The sound of shots.

The Prince is calm. "A gad. It will never be said that we were so pressed that we abandoned our meat." The Prince finishes his mutton as the others gather together what little they have left of their arms and possessions.

Donald, Young Donald, and Rory are making their farewells to the Prince.

"Alex. These men are to have one shilling for each day's service."

MacLeod takes out his purse. "How many days have you and your men been in service, Donald?"

Donald MacLeod counts on his fingers. "I make it fifty six, captain."

"Is it that long that we have been in friendship?"

"It is, your highness."

"Make it five pounds a man, MacLeod."

He leaves Captain MacLeod to count out the money.

The Prince addresses O'Sullivan. "How's you leg this evening?

"No better. Leave me with Captain MacLeod and I will make my own way in the world."

The Prince embraces O'Sullivan with great affection. "You have been my closest companion for so long, John. I don't know if I will survive without you."

"Nor I without you, sir." He starts to unbutton his blue tunic. "If you are captured, your name is Champville. You are a lieutenant in the Dauphine's Regiment of Foot.

The Prince stops him. "John.... I ask you? Would I pass for a French foot soldier?"

"Aye, it is a stretch of the imagination with that bonny face of yours."

Neil MacDonald cuts in. "Your highness, we must away!"

Ned pushes in. "Here's two shirts and a pair of stockings, master."

"I will miss you, dear friend."

"And I you, master." It is a moment of genuine warmth between master and servant.

"God protect you, Ned Burke."

O'Neil, meanwhile, is shaking O'Sullivan's hand. "See you in Paris, colonel." He steps back, clicks his heels, and salutes his friend.

O'Sullivan salutes back. "You are a devil of a man, Felix O'Neil. When we are back in Paris, the brandy is on you!"

"Yes, sir!"

"Come, sir, we must depart this instance" Neil leads the Prince and O'Neil away.

Captain MacLeod turns to Donald's party. "Away then, Donald, before you're caught."

"Good luck to you, young MacLeod."

Donald, Young Donald and Rory leave smartly, and disappear into the dark.

O'Sullivan is on his feet. "Well, young Captain, this beats Culloden for excitement. You think we can escape this time."

"Och aye, sir. We've been to Derby and back. They're no going to get us now. Ned!"

"Yes, master."

"You are now back in my service. I am not the Prince, but you are to strictly obey me."

"Do you think I've been spoiled during my time with the Prince? I've been right sorely abused, living in hovels, surviving near drowning, walking barefooted god knows how many miles. I am glad to be back in your service, sir."

"And I am glad to have you, Ned. Take the Colonel on your back, for there is no other way to get him off this island."

"Yes, sir." He offers his back to O'Sullivan. "Come, Colonel. I am used to transporting gentlemen."

MacLeod, and Ned with O'Sullivan on his back, departs the scene.

4

In the dark, the Prince, Neil, O'Neil, are making for the top of a hill that overlooks Lochboisdale.

"Are we followed?"

"C'est possible...." Neil replies.

The Prince is surprised. "Vous parlez francais?"

"Oui" He replies in French. "I studied for the priesthood at the Scots College in Paris."

"Your French is excellent."

"Thank you, sir. I have another confession."

O'Neil's eyebrows go up.

"I am in the service of the French government."

"As a spy?

"Under cover so to speak. My position as tutor to the MacDonald's has allowed me to promote Jacobite interests on the Long Island. Lady Clanranald, my chief provider, is a fine woman."

"Did you tutor MacDonald's sons?"

"I did. Ranald and Alexander take after their mother, but they have inherited some roguery from their father."

O'Neil joins in. "Are you in communication with France?"

"Yes, I have weekly despatch orders."

"How do you get them?"

"There is a dovecot at Nunton."

The Prince cheers enormously. "Why did you not reveal yourself before?"

"For obvious reasons. My orders are to help you escape, no-one else."

O'Neil gets his meaning. "Well, I'll be blasted. I'm expendable then, MacDonald?"

Neil gives him a non-committal look.

The sun is coming up. They are lying in the heather. The Prince is eating bread and cheese.

Neil is rearranging his plaid. "It is time to go." He picks up the provisions, his own gun and sword, the prince's fusee and one of his holsters. The Prince gathers his shirts, O'Neill his own linen.

As they were going on, the Prince claps Neil's shoulder.

"If we get free of our present troubles, I will make you live easy all your days in France."

"A nice French girl would be something. The Scots lassies are too fiery for me."

O'Neil puts in his view. "I'm quite partial to the Scots lassies. His lordship too. He took fair notice of a lass when he lay ill at Bannockburn."

"Now now, Felix. You are making me out to be a womaniser. Clementina Walkinshaw I know from childhood. She is named after my mother. Her father came out for my father in the Fifteen."

"I know you were quite taken by her. I'll be your best man at the wedding." O'Neil is trying to embarrass the Prince.

Charles ignores him. "Where are we headed?"

"We are on our way to meet one of my former pupils ... the prettiest girl in the Hebrides.

O'Neil's ears pick up. "Oh aye? What's her name?"

"She is a proper girl, Captain, and not for the likes of you. She is my cousin."

"Her name, man? Where's the harm?"

"Miss Flora MacDonald. Her stepfather Sir Hugh is in charge of the Militia on Benbecula."

"Man! You are playing with fire."

"Miss Flora is presently tending her brother's farm not far from here. Sir Hugh wants to send her back to Skye to be with her mother until the enemy are out of Uist."

"Are we the enemy, Neil?" The Prince is insecure.

"No, sir, with Captain Scott and his likes, no woman is safe."

"How does this interest us?"

"Sir Hugh proposes that the Prince travels with Miss Flora to Skye."

"The chief of the Benbecula Militia is helping us to escape?"

"Aye, he is."

"'Tis a tall tale, Neil."

"Not at all, sir. Sir Hugh will procure the necessary means to leave the island."

The Prince and O'Neil are equally troubled by the plan.

"The only person who does not know of the plan is Miss Flora."

O'Neil is indignant. "I've never heard such rot! Are you sane? This is worse than the Sinclairs from Orkney farce."

To Charles in French. "Will you trust me, sir? I am in the direct service of King Louis and my first charge is to make good your return to France."

The Prince is encouraged by Neil's statement "Oui. You have my complete confidence."

Neil, The Prince and O'Neil are a little way from the back of a small cottage silhouetted against a clear sky.

Neil goes into the house by an open window. Inside, there is a single candle burning. Neil creeps up to a bed, gently shakes it.

Flora, dark haired, fair skinned, twenty-four, startled, leaps upright.

"'Tis Neil, Flora."

"Neil MacEachain, you devil!"

"Is brother Angus at home?"

"No. He's away with the Militia."

"Good. I have brought a friend to see you."

Flora throws her legs over the edge of the bed. "At this hour? Is it the Prince?"

"It is."

Flora starts to dress quickly. She follows Neil into the parlour. She is barely half dressed when the latch of the cottage door is heard to click, and the Prince appears in the doorway.

"My, my. It is the Prince!"

"I am at your service, Miss MacDonald."

Flora lights another candle and places it on the wooden table dominating the parlour.

She indicates to the Prince to sit. O'Neil likewise sits.

Flora places a large bowl of cream in front of Charles. He takes his fill in two hearty go-downs. O'Neil takes the rest.

"Miss Flora, I am in imminent danger."

O'Neil butts in. "Is it in your power to convey the Prince to the Isle of Skye and your mother's house?"

Flora wide-eyed looks to Neil.

"It would be easy for you, Flora. Sir Hugh will give you a passport for yourself and a servant."

She looks to the Prince.

"I would disguise myself as your servant. Will you help me?"

Flora quietly looks at each of them in turn.

"Well?" Neil asks her.

Flora folds her arms. "With the greatest respect and loyalty, my answer is no."

Captain O'Neil is flabbergasted. "No???"

Neil is disappointed. "Flora!"

Flora is indignant. "Sir Hugh, my stepfather, is a captain in a regiment of militia commanded by Sir Alexander MacDonald. Sir Alex is one of the two great lairds in Skye ... whom with his wife, my aunt Lady Margaret, I am on the friendliest terms. My participation in this plot, if it became known, would be Sir Alex's ruin.

O'Neil is quick to counter. "No, not at all. Neil reports that Alexander is not at this time on Skye, he is in Fort August with the Duke of Cumberland ... the

Prince's cousin."

"The Duke of Cumberland and the Prince are currently not on friendly terms." Flora replies.

Neil smiles. "No, but there is no reason to think that by helping the Prince, the Duke will think that Alexander could be accused of connivance."

He pushes the plot along. "Sir Alex lives near the shore in Skye ... the Prince could be carried to his house and sheltered by Lady Margaret?"

O'Neil grins. "Think about the honour and immortality you would earn by so glorious an action?"

Their words have no effect on Flora. She remains cross armed and defiant.

The Prince now speaks for himself. "I do not underestimate the peril of what we ask you to do, Miss MacDonald. My friends have played the danger down. It is perilous beyond expectation. But I tell you, as a man who's life would be in your hands, it is an adventure so daring and audacious, it is dangerous beyond description."

Flora's grave but lovely eyes momentarily betray her joy at the prospect of danger. "Who's going to look after Angus's cattle?"

The men catch the sense that her reluctance is melting.

O'Neil pipes up. "Miss Flora. Do this deed and I will marry you!"

Her eyes flicker with contempt for O'Neil. "I will ask Lady Clanranald about the feasibility of the plan."

"And my marriage proposal?"

Hidden beneath the table, the Prince kicks O'Neil on the shin to shut him up.

Flora is mounted on a pony. There is enough moonlight to clearly see the track she will follow.

"I will send a boy to Hecla once I am at Lady Clanranald's."

Flora rides off in the moonlight.

"Where's Hecla?" the Prince asks.

Neil points upwards to a horn shaped mountain cast against the sky.

"Tis prudent to remove ourselves. From up there we can see half of South Uist and all of Benbecula."

It is morning. The bare wind swept mountain top of Hecla. They are on the summit proper, which consists of an overhanging lump of crag with spectacular views, especially towards the other main mountain, Ben More.

O'Neil is sleeping under an overhang. The Prince is lying under a large rock looking out across the island

"That is Corrodale down there? I recognise the lake."

"Aye, it is. Do you see those little red dots?"

Neil hands the Prince a spyglass. He puts his eye to it.

"Redcoats."

"Aye. Landed from those warships."

The Prince trains his eye on the ships.

"The Furness."

"Captain Ferguson." Neil taps the Prince on the arm. "Look over towards Ben More."

The prince trains his eye on the biggest mountain on the island, on the south side of the Corrodale valley.

"More Redcoats and militia men." The Prince lowers the spyglass.

"Scott's regiment, the 6th Foot."

The Prince leans back into a crevice. "Do you have any food?"

Neil hands him some bread and cheese."

"You've kept watch all night. Have Felix take his turn."

Neil wakes O'Neil.

The Prince is restless. He trains his spyglass in the other direction. He pans the hillside towards Benbecula.

"No-one has come for us."

"Flora is trustworthy beyond reproach." Neil replies.

"Then something has gone wrong. You will have to go to Clanranald's and find her."

Neil is tired. He is reluctant to do as he is ordered. "Tis a journey of thirty miles there and back."

"Be back by tomorrow noon or you will have my displeasure."

Neil does not protest. "As you wish, your highness." He gives his food and spare arms to O'Neil.

"Stay hidden." Neil sets off down the mountain.

O'Neil is softening towards the MacDonald. "That was harsh. He is a good man."

"This mountain is harsh. I don't want us to perish on it."

They watch as Neil bounds down the mountain.

In the main room of a small cottage, set out as a makeshift guard's house, a few MacDonald militiamen are lolling or standing.

Flora is sitting on a chair holding her shawl.

The door bursts opens. Sir Hugh MacDonald enters followed by Captain Ferguson. The militiamen on guard stand to attention and salute.

"Flora!" Sir Hugh is relieved to see her unharmed.

She rises in relief. "Father! They've kept me up all night!"

Sir Hugh is playing a part in front of Ferguson. "For mercy's sake, Flora, what were you doing crossing from Uist at midnight?"

"I was coming from Angus's farm."

"Did you not know that there's a curfew in the Uists?

"Tis a new thing. I know it now."

"Thank God you were arrested by my men and not Captain Scott's."

Ferguson rolls his eyes.

"Captain Scott is a fair man, Sir Hugh. These things you hear are exaggerated."

The militiamen in the room exchange looks with Sir Hugh. Sir Hugh gives the slightest movement of his head to indicate to his men to remain silent.

Ferguson is arrogantly strutting about.

"My men will take over the crossing guard. Lieutenant MacCaghan!"

"Benbecula is in my jurisdiction, Captain." Sir Hugh states forcefully.

"It was. Now, I am senior officer on the island." He shouts again. "Lieutenant MacCaghan!"

MacCaghan enters with a squad of weary Redcoats with fixed bayonets.

The militiamen look again to Sir Hugh for orders.

"I want these men and ever man under your command to be out looking for the Young Pretender!"

Sir Hugh turns to his men. "You heard the Captain's order."

The militiamen gather their weapons and plaids. They file out.

The tired Redcoats flop wherever they can. Ferguson is outraged. "Stand to attention in front of an officer!"

The Redcoats spring too. Flora is startled.

Sir Hugh addresses Flora. "It's no longer safe here, Flora. I'm sending you back to your mother in Skye."

"I am glad to go, father."

"Miss MacDonald will need a pass to leave the island." Ferguson states this in an off-hand manner. He has taken the bait.

"Yes, naturally, Captain."

Sir Hugh sits at a table and picks up a quill. "Which servants will you take with you, Flora?"

"Neil, and my maid....

Sir Hugh momentarily hesitates.

"... Betty Burke."

Sir Hugh shuffles in the chair. "Yes, Betty Burke..." He scribbles, and turns to hand the pass to Flora, but Ferguson snatches it from him.

Ferguson reads it. "Who is this Neil MacDonald?"

"My cousin. He is the Clanranald family tutor."

"Tutor, eh?" Ferguson snaps his fingers. MacCaghan leaves the room. "Half an hour ago we apprehended another MacDonald crossing from South Uist without a pass."

MacCaghan returns with Neil. His hands are bound.

Sir Hugh is immediately vociferous. "Captain Ferguson. This man is my nephew. Release him at once!"

"How many more kin do you have roaming at will without regard to the curfew?

"My kin have farm land on both sides of the crossing. It is imperative that they have free movement to carry out their tasks. They are all loyal to the King."

Ferguson pauses to consider the statement.

"Where were you coming from in South Uist?

"I was at Angus's farm. I heard gunshots. I was concerned for Miss Flora's safety."

Ferguson paces impatiently looking at the pass. He flicks his eyes. Neil is untied.

Flora is anxious. "I'll lodge with Lady Clanranald tonight, father. I have some needle work to finish before crossing to mother's."

Ferguson looks up. "Where is this Betty Burke now, Miss MacDonald?"

"She's at Lady Clanranald's."

"This Burke. She is from the Long Island?"

"No, sir, she is an Irish woman."

Ferguson appears satisfied. He hands Flora the pass.

"Take your man with you. I won't have it said that I do not care for your safety, Miss Flora."

"Thank you, Captain. Farewell, father. I will write from Mother's."

Flora and Neil leave.

Ferguson waves to MacCaghan. "Have the men stand at ease."

"Rest your arms, men." The Redcoats flop exhausted.

"Is Miss Flora your natural daughter, Sir Hugh?"

"My wife Marion's daughter. Her dead father was Clanranald's cousin."

"Clanranald! Clanranald! That is all I hear on this island. It concerns me that you MacDonald's are so closely related.

"Dear Captain, I am loyal to King George as is Flora. Marion's father was the Presbyterian minister of South Uist. You can rest assured, we have no love for the Stuart cause or their Tory politics."

The Prince is lying on his belly under the rock. He is watching the Redcoats sweeping across the moorland a mere two miles away. O'Neil is asleep.

"Felix!" O'Neil stirs. "What time have you?"

O'Neil awakes, takes out his pocket watch. He starts to rewind it. "This thing runs an hour fast every day. Lets guess ... two o'clock?"

The Prince turns his spyglass, scans the northern slope of the mountain. He stops. He sees Neil climbing up from below.

The Prince rises, creeps, runs half-bent down a long grassy ridge to intersect with the MacDonald. They meet two hundred feet below the summit.

"What news from Miss Flora?

"The plan is in place. She will join us tonight at Roisinis."

Neil indicates to the Prince to lie in the heather.

"Where is that?"

He points northwards "See yon mountain, that's Rueval. Benbecula means Mountain of the Fords. To the east of the mountain there are but a few peasants living a miserable life in the bog lands. Roisinis is the most easterly part. Tis hard to see it from here."

"How are we to make our way there?"

"By foot. The road crossing yonder to the west is now guarded by a detachment of Redcoats. They have placed sentries a gun shot length apart. We would be apprehended by wading across the shallows at low tide. We should wait for night."

"We cannot wait. The enemy from the south will be upon us. They are coming up the other side of this mountain."

Neil nods. "Wait here. I will fetch Captain O'Neil."

The Prince, Neil and O'Neil are lying in the heather near the edge of an inlet. A little way out from the shore, there are two Islanders fishing in a small boat.

"I know these men. They are MacDonalds." Neil whistles. The two fishermen look up. Neil stands.

One of the fisherman shouts to him in Gaelic. "Is it you, Neil."

"It is, Donal. Will you be fishing by Roisinis?"

The fishermen exchange looks. "And who'll be asking? Is it him that is from across the water?"

"It is, Donal. And there's a guinea in it for the fish."

The two fishermen are suddenly excited, but equally fully of fear. They row towards the shore.

The small boat with its five occupants drifts inshore on a flat craggy coast that has nothing to recommend it. There is no human habitation.

The Fishermen land them on the sand. Neil tries to pay them but they refuse. They take their leave.

The Prince sits down on a rock. He is completely exhausted from his week of exertion since leaving Corrodale. O'Neil, likewise falls to the sand exhausted.

"We must keep moving, your highness."

"I must rest." Charles removes himself from the rock, finds a grassy ledge and curls up in a ball to sleep.

Neil leaves them; strides purposefully to the top of a small rise and survey his surroundings. Inland is a ribbon of small lakes that stretch back towards the western side of Benbecula. Looking east, he takes a dozen strides to discover his way barred by an arm of the sea. Taking some steps to the north, he establishes that they have been landed on an island some twenty yards from the Roisinis shore. To make matters worse, some heavy clouds hanging overhead Rueval have descended on them, bringing heavy rain.

Neil wakes the Prince and O'Neil. "We have been landed on an island.

The Prince is tired, hungry and at his wits end. "Those devil MacDonalds! They have deliberately left us on this island to claim the reward!"

"They have made a mistake that is all."

"This is your doing, MacDonald! I have entrusted myself to you and now you have brought about my end!

"You are distressed through hunger, sir. I will strip off and swim to the other side ... find a boat."

Neil starts to strip, and is ready to make his swim when he notices a rock beginning to appear in the middle of the channel.

"See, sir! It is high tide. I think in time the water will fall and we can cross by foot.

The tide has gone out sufficiently for the three men to ford the channel barring their way to main part of Roisinis.

As they travel across the exposed peninsula, the terrain is a moor dotted with pools of water. There is no cover from the rain soaking them to the skin.

The Prince is conciliatory to Neil. "I am sorry, Neil. I am not myself today. In fact have not felt myself for considerable time now."

"None of us are ourselves at this time."

"The loss of my companions has upset me."

"You still have Mister O'Neil." Turns to him "Are you fine, Captain?"

O'Neil is shivering. He is too cold to answer. Instead he points ahead. There is a shieling not far off, and coming towards them dressed in seal-skins is an inquisitive Islander.

Neil steps forward to mask his view of the Prince. He speaks in Erse. "Can you comfort these poor Irish gentlemen who have escaped from Culloden?"

The Islander looks at him. It is obvious he knows nothing of recent events. However, he is curious to see who is with Neil and strains to look past him.

"Have you come to buy seal skins?"

"No, we are in need of shelter. They have not tasted meat for two days. We beg your charity."

"You can have fish." He turns and leads them towards the shieling.

The door of the hut is so low and narrow. The Prince is obliged to creep in on his belly as he did on Iubhard Island. The others quickly follow him inside.

Within ten minutes, they are feasting splendidly on butter and cheese. The Islander and his wife look at them with curious fascination. They have not experienced visitors many times in their lives.

Captain O'Neil is staring back at them. "They don't say much?

"They only know the root words of Erse. They have some other language they speak, a mixture of Norse and some forgotten Pictish tongue."

O'Neil grins at them. "You like my tunic. Yes, very expensive it is." The crofter offers sealskin in exchange for the tunic. "Not on your life, my beauty. Old O'Neil here doesn't want to be caught and hung as a rebel."

The Prince is surprised. "Is that the only reason you have kept that filthy thing?"

"It is, Charlie. If I'm caught I'm a proper prisoner of war in the pay of the French army. I'm just a soldier boy. Don't get me wrong. I have great affection for a Highland laddie like Neil, but it's not really my war, is it?"

"Even after all we have travailed?"

"Soldiering is my vocation. I don't know anything else. I have no convictions. I am a moral reprobate. Tis who I am."

"That's a damning testimony, Felix. I expected more of you?"

"I am a disappointment, sir."

"Not at all. I cannot fault you for your courage."

"I'd drink to that if we had anything other than milk."

O'Neil grins again at the two crofters still eyeing up his tunic.

The party of three are once more on their travels. The way is very bad. The Prince, despite the care Neil and O'Neil take of him, falls at almost every step in some hole or bog. When he loses a shoe in the mud, Neil, with vast trouble and pain, is obliged to put his hand up to his shoulder in the mud to retrieve it.

Then without warning, they arrive at the meeting place, a small shieling on the edge of a narrow sandy bay that faces North Uist.

The Prince and O'Neil are huddled in the rain.

Neil comes to them out of the dark. "The ladies have not come yet."

"Can we go into the house?"

"No. There's a section of militia men camped inside it.

"I am going mad! The enemy are everywhere!" He tears at his clothes in a kind of madness.

Neil is at a loss. "Mister O'Neil, I have no alternative but to send you to get Miss Flora."

"Where will I get a boat?"

"No, Captain. It is two hours that way to Nunton by the path. There, it starts right here. When you come to the crossways with the main highway, continue until you come near the sea. You cannot mistake Clanranald's. Tis the largest house on Benbecula."

"It sounds child's play after out recent trudging." O'Neil whispers to Charles. "Take heart, sir. We are not lost yet. Adieu!"

O'Neil disappears into the dark.

Neil picks the Prince up from the ground. "Come, there is a cow shelter nearby."

The sun is up. The Prince awakes to find a dirt-faced child cow-herder over him holding a bowl of milk.

Charles, sits up, drinks the milk. Neil is standing guard.

"The boy says the militia men come to the byre for their milk every morning. We will have to move off a little."

Charles hands the bowl back to the child.

The child smiles.

It is raining again and The Prince and Neil are huddled by a rock on the shore. The rock gives no shelter.

The morning slowly passes and the summer sun comes out. The air turns mild, and the damp sand releases its swarms of midges. Thereafter the Prince is in torment, crouched in his wet clothing, uttering little cries as the midges eat at him. Neil, more seasoned and hardened to life in the Uists, remains still, barely bothered by the hordes of gnats feeding on him.

Suddenly, the cowherd child appears, bids them to follow him to the shieling. Inside is empty, as the militiamen have decamped. An old woman, his grandmother, bids them to sit before a great peat fire.

The Prince, now attired only in his shirt, is turning his clothes before the fire in an effort to dry them. Neil seems untroubled by his wet clothes.

"Is Miss Flora coming, Neil?"

"She'll come whether Captain O'Neil gets through or not. There is a lovely little beach at Nunton on which Clanranald has a number of seaworthy boats. They will take one of these and come for us."

"Why is it taking so long?"

"As you said to Flora yourself, it is a dangerous enterprise. They may be watched for unusual signs of preparation. They must make their departure look what it should be, a departure to Skye to deliver Flora to her mother."

The Prince appears to be reassured.

"You know, sir, Mr. O'Neil is enamoured with Flora."

"She's a fine girl, Neil. Felix always has an eye for the ladies."

"She'll have nothing to do with him. She likes straight talking men.

"Like yourself, Neil."

"I could never have a lass like Miss Flora. She's too artful to find me interesting."

"Nonsense. You're the most intriguing of men. Women like mysterious men."

"I'll let you think that, sir." He beds down. "I think I need to sleep now. Keep watch, sir."

Neil closes his eyes. The Prince enjoys the heat of the fire.

It is night. The Prince and Neil are asleep. Two young MacDonald militia men with their red cross bonnets, Rory aged twenty, and John turned eighteen, enter the shieling carrying two bottles of wine and a dressed fowl.

The Prince and Neil rise in alarm, pistols cocked.

"Put down your pistols! Its Rory and John, Neil. We are sent by Flora to say Captain O'Neil is safe at Nunton."

The two boys remove their bonnets and bend their knees to the Prince.

"Up, lads. You are a welcome sight for my weary eyes."

The boys puff with pride.

John speaks excitedly. "The boat will come by the north channel into the little bay here. When it arrives, we are to go with you and Flora to Skye."

Rory is equally eager to spill the news. "Captain Ferguson ordered the rest of our company to search Hecla. They think you are still hiding in Corrodale!"

"Then we are fortunate to have left that mountain." comments the Prince.

John is full of information. "Miss Flora and Lady Clanranald have been busy day and night making Betty's' dress."

"What dress?" The Prince gives Neil a look.

"Have you not been told? You are to be Miss Flora's maid servant." John does not understand the Prince's ignorance of the plan. "Rory?"

"A Miss Betty Burke, your highness."

"Betty Burke? Is this a charade, Neil?"

"Tis Flora's notion. She said you would not be pleased to entertain the plan if you were told of it in advance."

Charles resigns himself. "I have no other plan, so why would I object to being dressed as a lady's maid. I think it's God's plan to ridicule me."

"Not at all, sir" Neil is tactful. "We must try all possible means to disguise your true person."

"Do we cross tonight?"

"Flora says it'll be tomorrow night." Rory confirms the Prince's worst fears. He throws himself down in front of the fire. He is very upset at the delay.

"They are making all haste, your highness." Rory is dismayed by the Prince's behaviour. Charles sees the look, pulls himself together.

"I apologise for my ill-humour, gentleman. I thank you for all you have done." He holds up the fowl. "Let's feast, drink and be merry."

The MacDonalds join Charles by the fire. The young cowherd keeps watch with his grandmother at the door.

It is a warm summer's night. The sky is ablaze with all of the northern stars. The Prince is now standing in the doorway admiring the vastness of the skyline stretching across the Minch to Skye.

Rory MacDonald, taking his turn to stand guard on the headland gives out a shout. It is Flora's party.

The Prince and Neil go down to the small sandy bay. Soon the sound of oars is clearly heard and out of the gloom, Flora's boat party appears in the inlet.

The Prince is cheered. "Get the old lady to stoke the fire, Neil. Our company will need refreshment."

The sun is up. Flora, Lady Clanranald, her daughter Peggy aged seven, O'Neil and the Prince are dining in the smoke-filled hovel.

Neil is standing guard in the doorway, while MacDonald boys are keeping company with the two boatmen who have brought the party to Roisinis.

Inside, the conversation is jovial. Lady Clanranald, a good-looking woman in her mid-forties, is enthralled at meeting Charles.

"I am so pleased at last to have met your highness. I have had so many messages about your being here, and going there, that I am pleased that we have helped you to outwit these beasts trying to end your life."

"Lady Clanranald. From Neil I have heard that you have been my saviour and protector."

"I ask you to forgive my rogue of a husband who has gone to the mainland. I don't know what you have made of his blowing hot and cold. My worry is for my sons. Is there no news of them?"

There is awkwardness at the mention of Ranald and Alexander. They did not cover themselves with glory at Culloden by deserting the field.

"We would have had news had they been captured, mother."

"You are right, Peggy."

The Prince is courteous. "We must think the best ... that perhaps Ranald and Alexander are taking refuge in the hills with Cluny MacPherson or his ilk."

"I don't think I will ever have them home again."

They fall silent.

Flora takes out a paper. "Here is our pass to Skye." She shows it to the Prince. "Myself, Neil and Betty Burke."

O'Neil is vexed. "You have deceived me, Miss MacDonald? Where is my pass? You mentioned nothing of this on the way here."

"Miss MacDonald. Captain O'Neil must journey with us."

"The man cannot speak the language of the country. If he is interrogated, he would give us all away with his broad brogue."

"You astound me! What will I do if I do not go with the Prince?"

Lady Clanranald interjects on Flora's behalf. "You are a man of fortune, Mister O'Neil. You will make your own luck."

"I am as wanted as the Prince, madam. I would say my luck has run out."

"I will not embark unless Felix is by my side!" The Prince is up on his feet.

The assembled company looks at the Prince as if he is mad. O'Neil realises that the Prince cannot have his way.

"Miss Flora is correct, sir. I am a grave risk to the venture. You must assent to go with her, or I will instantly go off on my own. I am indifferent to what becomes of myself unless you are safe."

Lady Clanranald is heartened. "You are the first sensible Irishman I have encountered."

"You flatter me, madam. There are no sensible Irishmen."

"Then the matter is settled." Flora looks squarely at O'Neil. "I have changed my opinion of you, Mister O'Neil."

"Well, thank you, Miss Flora. That is the first kind word I have had from you."

"Then it is well, Mister O'Neil, as we are not likely to meet again."

"My, Flora, you know how to wound a man. Tis my loss, and the Prince's gain."

Flora blushes.

It is late afternoon. A young MacDonald messenger is running towards the bothy. He speaks with the MacDonald brothers.

Neil hastily enters the bothy with Rory MacDonald. He addresses Lady Clanranald.

"General Campbell is on Benbecula with fifteen hundred men. After you left last night, an advance party headed by Ferguson broke into Nunton House, and requisitioned it!"

"The man slept in Lady Margaret's bed!" Rory announces in disbelief.

Lady Clanranald rises in an instant. "I must make haste by foot!"

Neil stays Lady Clanranald by the arm. "Auntie. Our plotting has been discovered. Captain Scott is also now in Benbecula. Come with us to Skye?"

"No, Neil. I have Peggy to consider. Too many fine Uist houses have gone up in flames and their possessions scattered. Mine will not be one of them. Farewell, your highness.

Lady Clanranald kisses his hand. She takes Peggy by the hand and hurries out of the bothy.

"I'll go with them to within sight of the house."

The Prince embraces O'Neil. "Adieu, old soldier."

"Au revoir, sir."

O'Neil rushes out in pursuit of Lady Clanranald and her attendants.

The Prince turns to Flora. "My life is in your hands, Miss MacDonald."

Flora pulls from a trunk a floral dress with embroidered sprigs. "Its a bonny dress, your majesty. It took two days and nights to alter it for you."

The Prince takes stock of his new costume.

"And you'll have to be wearing this bonnet to hide that hairy face."

"I'll shave myself clean, Flora."

"It is well then that you will be Miss Burke, my serving girl. However, I have no design to order you to do my biding."

"Thank you, Flora. I'm sure you would be a fine mistress if you did."

Flora lowers her head in modesty. "Then I will leave you, sir, to your change."

The Prince panics. "Surely you will stay to help me, Flora. I have no idea how a maid attires herself."

Flora is slightly exasperated. "Och, you are such a fickle man as any I've known."

Charles smiles, starts to remove his waistcoat.

The Prince is now dressed as Betty Burke and dusk is falling. He is an unwomanly sight. He cannot hide his manly gait as Neil, Flora, and the two MacDonald boys, make their way to the shoreline.

As the combined party round the shore to join the two MacDonald oarsmen, four boats with armed Redcoats come into view at the mouth of the inlet. They have not as yet seen the party on the beach.

The Prince and his companions throw themselves down into the sand dunes. The Redcoats continue across the inlet.

"They must have rowed from Nunton."

"How long does that take?" asks the Prince.

"Two, maybe three hours depending on the tide. Lady Clanranald can barely have reached home by now."

"So they still do not know we are here?"

The Redcoat boats slip from view behind the headland.

They slowly rise to their feet. Neil grimaces. "If Ferguson extracts a confession from my aunt then they'll be a thousand Redcoats running along the track to this beach within the hour."

Flora is brushing sand from her dress. She seems quite unconcerned for her own safety. "Tis half an hour till dark. We must clear the inlet in the daylight to avoid the rocks."

The Prince takes charge. "Then we cannot delay. We must depart now and pray that the Redcoats we just saw will not be in sight when we round the headland."

There is a swarm of military activity at Nunton House. Lady Clanranald and Peggy enter the drawing room to find Captain Ferguson and General Campbell sitting in her large comfortable chairs. They are surrounded by a number of other Officers.

They all rise.

Captain Ferguson is the first to speak. "Good evening, my lady."

"Good evening, gentlemen." She is cross about the intrusion into her house.

Campbell is a gentleman. "Forgive me, Lady Clanranald, but there simply was no other house large enough to accommodate my staff. I am Major General Campbell. We are hunting for the Young Pretender."

"I've heard. Peggy, go upstairs."

"No, mother. I'm staying with you."

Ferguson eyes the child then turns to Lady Clanranald. "When we arrived, there was no one here but servants. Where is your husband, madam?"

"He is on clan business in Knoydart. There is concern for his property there."

"And your sons, madam?"

"As you know, they foolishly disobeyed their father to follow the Stuart cause. I know not where they are or how they are."

The General is sympathetic. "Many of our finest families have been ripped asunder by this business, Lady Clanranald."

"And they must pay for it, General!" Ferguson is devoid of feeling. "MacDonald of Boisdale is your husband's brother?"

"He is."

"Do you know why we arrested him?"

Lady Clanranald shakes her head and pulls Peggy close to her skirts. Ferguson smiles insincerely.

"Come, come, madam. You know fine why we have him aboard my ship?"

"I do not?"

"He has given succour to the fugitive! How do you call him? Bonnie Prince Charlie?"

"I have heard him called that by the servants."

Ferguson presses home his questioning. "Where have you been, madam? I slept in your empty bed 'til eight o'clock this morning."

Lady Clanranald tries to hide her disgust at having Ferguson sleep in her bed. "I have been sitting up all night and this day with a sick child."

"What is the name of the child?"

"Betty. The child is much improved."

"That is a pretence to cover the real purpose of your journey!"

Campbell is annoyed by Ferguson's tone. "Captain Ferguson! This is Lady Clanranald's own house."

"It is, sir, but I am arresting the said Lady for helping the Young Pretender to escape. She has supplied him with a boat."

"Is this true, madam?"

Lady Clanranald does not reply.

"It as I said, sir, the whole island has been assisting him!" Ferguson signals MacCaghan. "Take her aboard the Furness!

"Mama!" Peggy fears the worst for her mother.

Lady Clanranald is taken out. Peggy tries to run after her but is blocked by Ferguson.

"Leave me alone!" She struggles to break free of Ferguson's grip. "Mama!"

Ferguson slaps her hard across the face.

The child falls to the floor.

General Campbell is enraged. "Enough!"

"Do you want to catch the Young Pretender, General?"

Campbell remains silent.

"Why don't we ask the child where he is?"

Ferguson closes the drawing room doors.

5

The Prince, Neil, Flora, two MacDonalds, two Oarsmen. They are rowing out into the Minch.

They are fearful of discovery. Each scans the shoreline for pursuing boats.

The light is dropping and there is little or no breeze.

They leave the Benbecula shore behind, and once darkness falls, they feel it is safe enough to hoist the sail and catch the breeze to send them on their way to Skye.

It is many hours later and the Prince is singing 'Twa Bonnie Maidens' to entertain Flora. His voice fills the void of the night.

"Il y a deux jeunes filles, ou bien trois jeunes filles, Qui passent le Minch, qui passent la mer ...."

Flora is asleep and the Prince keeps watch over her, holding in place a plaid to protect her from the sea spray.

Midway across the Minch, the wind picks up. The boat starts to pitch and weave through the surging waves. The Prince is happy and content. He is no longer afraid of the ocean that he crossed some two and half months before in his flight from Moidart. The Long Island is behind him, and whatever happens when they reach Skye, he has made his escape from near certain capture. His luck has changed. He is no longer a fugitive but a free man. He has survived many trials and now there is the hope that he may still get aboard a ship for France.

He is a Stuart, and his tutor Sheridan has taught him to never give up. Never!

It is the morning of the twenty eighth of June and a thin early mist lies on the calm sea near the shore of Skye. To the south, the mountains of the Cuillins, so rarely free of snow; rise against the clear blue sky.

The boat beaches on the rocky shore so that the members of the party may relieve or refresh themselves. They are tired from a sleepless night. Flora, by comparison, is fresh and high-spirited. Hiding from possible view under the cliffs, she prepares breakfast for them in her own efficient way. The MacDonald boys collect drinking water from a spectacular hanging waterfall and bring it to her to share with the party. They are all in good fettle, and happy to have made the crossing without mishap.

Once more, they are on the sea, and making headway towards Uig bay. As they round the cliff at Vaternish, two Militia sentries are gazing down at them from the cliff top.

"Boatman! Pull to shore! Pull to shore!"

They are well within musket range of the sentries. Neil shouts at the boatmen "Veer to port!"

The boatmen take immediate action; turn the craft away from the cliffs and towards the open bay.

The Militiamen pick up their muskets.

The boat is now being dashed by waves, as it is side on to the wind. The waves slap against the boat.

The Militiamen take aim

The Prince pushes Flora to the bottom of the boat and covers her with his body.

The first sentry fires. His shot is well wide.

Flora sits upright. "I will not have you cover me like this! Tis you we must protect!"

The second sentry is a better marksman. The sail is holed by his shot.

"This is no time to argue, Flora! Get yourself down!"

A third shot zips in the water.

The Oarsmen and the MacDonald brothers are now rowing away strongly. They are now beyond the range of the sentries' muskets.

Flora steals a look to the cliff. The sentries are running to a pair of horses.

"They were MacLeods. They'll report to MacLeod at Dunveggan."

"Don't be afraid, Flora. We will not be taken."

"Tis a time like this we could be having Donald MacLeod with us."

"Donald the pilot?"

"Aye, he is my first cousin Catherine's husband."

"Another MacDonald?"

"The daughter of my father's sister who is a Glenaladale."

"I am forever surprised by the inter-marriages of the MacDonalds. Are Rory and John cousins as well?"

"They are younger cousins, of course."

"And our two boatmen?"

"John is a MacMurich, and Duncan a Campbell."

"Not related then?"

"Both married to cousins of mine."

The Prince laughs, "Then I am the only one in this boat not related to you!"

"Oh, I wouldnae say that. Somewhere in my body there'll be a bit of Stuart."

The Prince laughs even louder. Flora smiles sweetly.

The crags of the Quirang tower above them. The boat party disembarks on Monkstadt beach. Flora and Neil prepare to set out.

"You are leaving me here?"

"I must visit Lady Margaret alone and speak privately with her." Flora addresses the MacDonalds. "Cousins. If anyone comes you are to tell them that she is your cousin's maid and a lazy creature of little worth."

They nod.

The Prince frowns.

Flora and Neil depart.

It is an hour later and Neil returns. He calls the men together and begins to pay them for their night's work. The Prince sits quietly on a rock with his head in his hands. Rory comes to him.

"Are you leaving?"

"Aye, the boat has to be returned." Rory steps forward to pay his respects. The Prince's offers his hand, but suddenly remembers that he is disguised as Betty Burke, and withdraws it quickly.

"God be with you, Rory."

"God be with you, your highness."

Rory joins his brother to push the boat back into the water. They leap in and join the two boatmen. They gaze back as they drift out into the bay.

"Where are they going?"

"Back to Nunton."

"It is folly, Neil. They'll be taken the moment they land, and spill all."

"It would be the same outcome if they were taken here. We have a day's grace by sending them home."

"You are deliberately sending them to be captured?"

"I have a duty to do all I can to preserve you."

Neil walks the Prince up the shoreline to the back of a small hillock.

"Am I not going up to the house?"

"Lady Margaret said that she'd not see your highness dressed like a woman."

"She does not want to receive me?"

"No, sir. You must wait here."

"It is Hecla all over again."

"No, sir, it is not. I promise I will be back before an hour has passed."

Neil goes off.

Flora and Lady Margaret, a beauty to rival Flora, and Marion MacDonald of Kirkibost, are entertaining Lieutenant MacLeod and some of his MacLeod Militia men in Monkstadt House.

MacLeod is totally smitten by Flora. Lady Margaret is nervously looking out of the window.

"Is something amiss, Lady Margaret?"

"Not at all, John. I'm keeping an eye on the weather."

"I'm keeping my eye on Miss Flora. I fear I should be searching her boat."

"Come, John, I'm Sir Hugh's step daughter. Surely your commission does not compel you to search every boat?"

"No, Miss Flora, you are right there."

Marion MacDonald interjects. "Lieutenant MacLeod searched my boat top to bottom yesterday."

"It is my duty to search every boat on a Saturday, but I am not compelled to do it on a Sunday."

"I take it you are either a very religious man, or you are frightened you might find the Young Pretender pressed to my planks?"

"Now that would be a find!"

There is a knock on the door.

Lady Margaret goes out.

An old man, MacDonald of Kingsburgh, is standing hopping from one foot to the other. By his side is Neil, holding a bundle of folded shirts.

"Kingsburgh! For Sir Alex's sake I have to avoid all contact with The Prince!"

"I understand, my lady."

"Have you sent the letter to Donald Roy?"

"Yes, my lady."

"We are all respectable members of the Church of Scotland and sober supporters of the Government, but at heart, Kingsburgh, I'm a Jacobite."

"Yes, my lady."

"Take the Prince to your house and in the morning hand him over to Donald Roy in Portree. He'll pass him on to the MacLeod's of Raasay who will take him to the mainland." She turns to Neil. "Come with me. You just have to get Flora away from that young MacLeod."

Neil dumps the shirts in Kingsburgh arms and follows Lady Margaret into the room.

The Prince is lying flat in the grass staring up at the sky. He is chewing on a piece of grass. He hears something that makes him turn and get on his elbows. Ahead, a man clutching a bottle of wine is staggering towards him. As he nears him, Charles jumps up to hit him with a large stick.

"How now, your highness! Stay!" Kingsburgh exclaims. "Tis your humble servant Kingsburgh, Lady Margaret's estate manager."

The Prince lowers the stick. Kingsburgh runs his eyes up and down the Prince's attire.

"Tis worse than I imagined."

The Prince is not amused. "Is the lady ready to receive me?"

"Oh no, your highness. For her husband's sake she has to avoid any personal association with you. I have been sent by her to take you to my house."

"How far is it?"

"Tis only seven miles."

The Prince is weary, tired and cold. "I am to walk seven miles in this foolish attire?"

"Tis a flat road."

"These shoes will not suffice any distance." He raises his dress and shoes Kingsburgh his worn our shoes."

"My, you have had a sojourn, your majesty. I will replace them for you."

"You have a pair of shoes for me?"

"Seven miles that way, your majesty."

The Prince is resigned to the seven-mile walk.

Unseen, Neil appears. He whistles to gain their attention, waves to Kingsburgh that all is clear.

The Prince takes a swig of wine. "Is Flora coming with us?"

"Miss Flora will meet us at my house. Come, let us walk."

The Prince follows Kingsburgh. They join with Neil, cross some fields, and start down the carriage-wide Portree road towards Kingsburgh.

It is one hour later. Kingsburgh, Neil and 'Betty' are straddling the road. The Prince's gait is ungainly and as his toes are sticking out of his shoes, he is hobbling, as the road is stony.

"This is a devil of a journey!"

"Tis a devil you are, Betty Burke!" Neil replies. "Not a mile without a dozen complaints."

Kingsburgh is astounded at Neil's boldness with the Prince "You treat him roughly, Neil."

"I am keeping him going, Alex. Tis a public highway and he is an odd looking female. He is drawing long looks from the crofters."

They are beginning to leave behind the many fields that have lined the road since Monkstadt as the road rises to follow the cliff top south of Uig. The Prince has quietened down and they are making steady progress now, being just under halfway to Kingsburgh's house.

In short time, coming up behind them on ponies is Flora, accompanied by Marion MacDonald and her eighteen-year-old maid Mairi.

The Prince turns and sees them coming on. "Who's that with Flora?"

"Marion MacDonald, another relative of Miss Flora's from North Uist. Be careful, she knows the Prince is expected in Skye."

The riders come up on them.

Marion MacDonald, curious at the strange woman, trots along beside the Prince and bends down to have a look at Betty's face. The Prince hides it from her.

"Your servant is shy, Flora."

The Maid is less shy. "I never saw a woman of more impudent appearance! In my opinion she is either Irish or a man in female dress."

"Hold your tongue, Mairi!"

They are crossing a small stream. Betty lifts her skirts indecently high.

Mairi is shocked. "Look at her, Miss Flora! Do you observe her! Curse the wretch! Is that not a muckle step for a woman? I never saw a maid manage her skirts so badly!" Mairi addresses the Prince sternly. "Where are you from, woman???

Flora puts her pony between the Maid and the Prince. "She is an Irish maid whom I acquainted in Stornoway. Isn't that right, Marion?"

"Is it, Flora?" She realises that Betty is the Prince. "Oh, yes, it is. Famed for her..." She is lost for words at being in the presence of the Prince.

"Upon report of her being a famous spinner of lint. I have engaged her for my mother's household in Armadale."

Flora takes the reins of Mairi's pony.

"Miss Flora!"

"Tis certain to rain, Mairi. Tis best we hurry." She pulls Mairi's pony along. "Come, Marion, let us canter a little faster, and leave Kingsburgh and my servants to follow on."

Flora kicks her pony and Mairi is made to follow. Marion kicks, and pursues them.

The Maid looks back and sticks her tongue out at 'Betty'.

Kingsburgh strikes to the right, and leaves the road. He leads the Prince and Neil on a small track across an open piece of moor land. Coming the other way is a middle-aged man and a young woman, by her looks his daughter. They are attired in their best clothes as if they have been on important business after church.

Between them is a small stream. Neil turns back to address Betty. "For God's sake, sir, take care of your walk, or you will be discovered."

The Prince laughs. "Thank you for your concern, Mr. MacDonald." He crosses a stream, and lets his petticoats trail in the water.

Neil is angry, but Kingsburgh takes him by the arm. "Let it go, my boy. We will soon be there."

The man passes, raises his hat to Kingsburgh.

"May the Lord bless you, Alex."

"And bless you, Alistair, and Miss MacNeil."

The man nods to Neil, while Miss MacNeil stares at the strange creature in the dress and bonnet. She makes no comment, and passes on with her father.

The Prince admonishes his companions. "Gentlemen, if I wished to be found out, then I would go about naked. Please stop chiding me."

Kingsburgh is soft spoken. "All we ask, your highness, is your help to conceal your person. Tis your well-being we have concern for, not ourselves."

"Point taken, sir. I have been wrong to act so foolishly. Forgive me."

Kingsburgh and Neil nod their acceptance of the apology.

Kingsburgh House is a substantial house with a large hall. Neil is settled on a high-back chair. The Prince is pacing up and down the hall in his female disguise. Kingsburgh enters the hall with Mrs Kingsburgh, a homely sixty-year old.

The Prince goes to her, salutes her, kisses her hand. "Madam..."

She pulls back in dread, rushes out of the hall into a back room. Kingsburgh rushes after her, and brings her back.

"My dear, this is the Prince."

"The Prince!" She swoons. Kingsburgh and the Prince catch her. "We are ruined and undone forever! We will all be hanged!"

"Wife, we all die but once. If we hang for this, we die in a good cause. Please, go make some supper, eggs, butter, cheese."

"What supper is that for a Prince? "

"Madam, it will be a feast for me. You little know how I have been living of late."

The Prince and Kingsburgh are settled by a glorious fire. Mrs. Kingsburgh is coming and going with all manner of provisions. Neil keeps watch by the window.

Kingsburgh hands the Prince a fresh pipe. The Prince admires it. "What I would have done in Corrodale for a pipe like this."

Kingsburgh pours him a glass of wine, hands it to him. "Tis a lucky thing I was at Lady Margaret's. I had no design to be there on a Sunday. What would you have done if I had not come?"

"You could not avoid being there. Providence ordered you to be there on my account."

Kingsburgh reaches and removes Betty's headdress. "That is better, sir, much better.

Mrs Kingsburgh re-enters with a tray of plates. She gasps. "You are very much sunburnt, your highness, but not scabbed to the eyeholes as the Hanoverians put out about you."

"Is that what they are saying? My legs are hacked in some parts from sleeping in wet hose. But look..." he rolls up his sleeves "... most of me is still whiter than your purest ladies."

Mrs Kingsburgh takes a close look. "Indeed, your highness, such bonny, clean white skin like Miss Flora."

"Is Miss Flora arrived?"

"She's resting upstairs, sir. She came an hour afore you."

"Then stir her and have her share supper with us."

Mrs. Kingsburgh goes out.

Kingsburgh knocks back his wine. "Flora's a fine lass. You should have seen how she dealt with that Lieutenant MacLeod. But she's got her eye on my son Allan. Isn't that right, Neil?"

"Aye."

"He's a drover. A fine big lad. He's away driving Sir Alex's cattle to England.

The Prince is slightly surprised. "I'm glad to hear that commerce is continuing amidst the strife."

"Sadly, it is. All the confiscated goods and cattle. They're selling everything at knock down prices in Glasgow."

Kingsburgh fills their glasses liberally. He begins to sing.

"Green sleeves and pudding pies, Tell me where my mistress lies, And I'll be with her before the rise, Fiddle and aw' together. May our affairs abroad succeed, And may our king come home with speed, And all pretenders shake for dread, And let HIS health go round. "

Flora enters the room with Mrs. Kingsburgh. She is freshly dressed and washed. The Prince rises. Mrs. Kingsburgh scolds her husband.

"You old Jacobite! You'll wake the servants! Be seated, your highness!"

She waves him to sit at the table laid out for supper. The Prince pulls out a chair for Fiona to sit on his right, then for Mrs. Kingsburgh on his left. Neil and Kingsburgh sit opposite.

"It is awhile since I have sat at a table and enjoyed such civil company. May I say grace?"

"Is that the Catholic grace, your highness?" Mrs. Kingsburgh enquires timidly.

"It is. Is there something the matter?"

Kingsburgh interjects "We are all Protestants, sir. Except Neil."

Neil nods.

The Prince is accommodating. "Then I will make up my own grace so that none in offended." He closes his eyes. "Lord, may we count our blessings despite all the hardships thrown upon us, and cherish true companionship and the love of those around us. Amen."

Kingsburgh "Very well said, your highness."

"I was quite religious as a lad. The Pope was my godfather ... a great supporter of my father. My brother Henry is a Cardinal."

"My grandfather was a Presbyterian minister, but time, in general, can only inform us what is good, and what is bad religion." Flora settles herself.

"Did you tutor Flora in these thoughts, Neil?"

"No, sir, Flora has come to these notions herself."

Flora smiles sweetly at Neil. "After my lessons with Neil, I was sent to school in Edinburgh for three years. It quite broadened my horizons."

"Edinburgh is such a wicked place!" Mr. Kingsburgh realises she has spoken out of turn and is embarrassed. The others laugh.

"I'm a Highland lass, but I've a fancy for better things. I'd like Allan to settle with me in the Carolinas."

"Another for America? The Prince asks.

"Is it wrong to want your own land and be far away from kings?

Mrs. Kingsburgh "Flora!

The Prince dismisses the objection. "Let her speak. Are you a republican, Flora?

"I am inclined that way, though now that I have dined with a prince, I may not be accepted by my own as a free thinker."

"I sincerely apologise for that." Charles replies.

"Oh I don't suppose it will really matter. I will just pretend to others that I did not enjoy myself when I was with you."

Mrs. Kingsburgh again. "Flora MacDonald!"

The rest of the company laughs heartily.

Mrs. Kingsburgh is holding on to Flora. She has a pair of scissors in her hand. She knocks on a door.

Inside the room, the Prince is sitting on a grand bed. The bed is unmade as he dresses back into his female disguise.

On the other side of his door, Mrs. Kingsburgh is quite animated and is embarrassing Flora.

"I am requesting Miss MacDonald to come and help you dress."

The Prince is fiddling with his cap. "Tell her to come in. She knows me well enough now."

The door opens. Flora enters alone with the scissors hidden behind her back.

He gestures her to sit on a chair by the bedside. "Can you help me with this cap?" He bends down on one knee, puts his hands around her waist, and puts his head in her lap.

Mrs. Kingsburgh is at the doorway. She calls in Gaelic. "Get a lock of his hair!"

In Gaelic. "No, I will not!"

"What is she asking?"

"She wants a lock of your hair as a keepsake."

"Cut away, Miss MacDonald. I owe you the head on which this hair rests. It will be eternally grateful."

Flora is momentarily moved. She closes her eyes and cuts a lock. Mrs. Kingsburgh watching from the doorway is gleeful. Flora looks down at him – his head is still in her lap.

"I am done. May I help you with your cap now?"

Charles raises his head. Flora adjusts his cap on his head.

"I must look very unwomanly in these clothes?"

"I will admit that Miss Burke has aroused some comments. Kingsburgh has procured some gentlemen's clothes for you. You can change into them once you are clear of the house. There, we are done."

The Prince gets up. Flora picks up the lock of hair.

"I would be honoured if you kept some of that lock for yourself. A token of our friendship."

Neil is waiting by the main door as Charles comes down the stairs with Flora. A young boy aged fourteen, Sandy MacQueen stands in the hall with his bonnet in his hand.

Flora and Neil say their farewells to Kingsburgh and his wife and depart.

The Prince looks at his toes protruding out of his brogues.

Kingsburgh smiles and lifts high a pair of brogues. The Prince's eyes light up.

"I said I would have a pair of shoes for you. These are Allan's, and I think they'll fit."

Charles quickly discards his old shoes and puts on the new brogues. "They are a fit, sir, a wonderful fit!"

Kingsburgh picks up the Prince's discarded footwear. "I will keep these till you are installed in London. I will reintroduce myself by shaking them at you, to remind you of your night under my roof."

"I will keep you to that promise, Kingsburgh." He turns to his wife. "Madam." He kisses her hand.

She blushes

Kingsburgh gatherers a length of plaid over his arm and they allow themselves to be led out by Sandy.

They are in a wood and Sandy is keeping watch.

The Prince has thrown off his female attire. He is finishing putting on a tartan short coat and waistcoat, with a philibeg and short hose.

Kingsburgh hands him the plaid, a wig and a blue bonnet. "My son Allan is a bonnie dresser."

Charles embraces Kingsburgh. "I thank you. I will not forget your service."

Kingsburgh shrugs it off. "You are expected at the Portree Inn at eight o'clock. God bless you."

Sandy is leading the Prince up out of the Snizort valley and on to the hills to avoid the well used road to Portree.

The view across Raasay to the Torridon Hills on the mainland is glorious.

"Tis a fine summer's day, Sandy."

"Aye, sir." He points. "It is to Raasay and then to Applecross on the continent that has been planned for you."

"The continent?"

"Aye, sir, the continent of Scotland."

"Oh I see." The Prince smiles at the boy. "MacKenzie country."

"Aye, sir." They reach the brow of the hill. "That is Portree below, sir."

A pall of smoke hangs over a collection of a hundred or more thatched hoses nestled by a horseshoe bay.

"We are to wait here until evening."

The boy sits himself down in the long grass. The Prince follows suit. The boy unwraps a parcel of cheese, butter and bread. He offers the Prince to share with him.

"No, not at all, Sandy. You feast."

"No, sir, this is for you, not for me. I had my porridge this morning."

The Prince is moved by the humbleness of the lad.

"Then we will share it. We are two gentlemen on the road together. It is only right that we dine together."

The boy looks at the Prince in admiration. "Are you really Bonnie Prince Charlie?"

Charles "I am, but not so bonnie now."

"I think you're unco bonnie in uncle Allan's clothes."

"Sandy, you are a flatterer! You will go far in the world!"

Sandy smiles.

Flora, Neil and Captain Donald Roy, thirty-eight, with a wounded left foot, are in a booth in the Portree Inn. They are very familiar with one another, as only close family can be.

"This sodden foot! I don't know hardly a man who

didn't get a grapeshot wound at Culloden!"

"Have you news of Ranald and Alexander? Lady MacDonald thinks them dead?"

"Ranald's eloped with MacKenzie's daughter."

"What?

"The Earl of Seaforth's lass. They've run off to France. They're enjoying love under the name of Mr and Mrs Black!"

Neil is indignant. "Its a disgrace. After ordering the MacDonald's not to fight at Culloden, leaving the field without firing a shot?"

"The Macdonald's have been on the King's right since Bannockburn!"

"Donald. Keep it down..."

"I've been riding all over this sodden island, Flora, trying to keep the peace. Lady Margaret had a fit when the Prince showed up on Sir Alex's lands."

"You're a fugitive yourself, Donald Roy. Wanted by the Redcoats as much as the Prince."

"Don't you admonish me, lassie."

Neil tries to get Donald to see reason. "Every MacDonald on the Long Island has stuck their neck out for the Prince. Even your sister Catherine."

"She's no sister of mine. She married yon Campbell!"

"Donald Campbell saved the Prince from a mob who wanted to take him for the reward."

Donald Roy contemplates the scene described to him. He becomes conciliatory. "Well, I'm no ashamed I didn't come to present my services to the Prince when you landed at Monkstadt. I just couldn't face seeing him dressed as yon Betty Burke!"

The landlord MacNab, a thin faced man of forty-five, approaches. "There's a boy looking for you?"

Sandy appears from behind MacNab as he lumbers off.

Sandy addresses Donald in Gaelic. "The gentleman's waiting outside, uncle."

"A gentleman you say?" Donald Roy gives his companions a wink.

Flora "Tarry not. This is your chance to be of service."

Donald Roy shuffles to his feet. "You're a devil of a woman, Flora MacDonald."

Donald follows Sandy out.

It is raining hard. The Prince looms out of the dark. "Donald Roy!"

"Your highness!"

"Are you injured, Captain?"

"Gun shot through the foot. Got hit just before the dragoons broke the left flank."

"Is it safe to enter?"

"Aye. Be careful. If you are asked, you are a Mister Thompson of Edinburgh."

Inside the inn, the Prince is standing. His clothes are soaking wet. Donald pours him a dram. He downs it in one gulp.

"You're a thirsty man, Mister Thompson?"

"Aye. Another please."

Donald pours him another. Sandy enters again, speaks to Donald Roy.

"You're wanted by another gentleman."

"Oh aye ...?" Donald Roy follows Sandy outside.

The Prince slides in snug besides Flora and Neil.

"I'm sorry for getting you out in the rain, Flora?"

"I'm used to the mist."

The Prince toasts Flora and Neil, downs another dram.

Donald re-enters in a wet state. He sits down. "The MacLeod's have agreed to wait until the rain slackens."

"I have time to eat?"

"Och aye. Lets have a dram as well."

The Prince smiles at Flora. She is surprised at the Prince's capacity for alcohol.

Donald Roy signals to MacNab.

Neil hands the Prince a parcel "A change, sir."

"Another outfit ruined, I'm afraid, Neil." The Prince indicates the rain has ruined the clothes he is wearing.

"Aye, you've been through a few garments in your travels with me."

"We'll make Allan some others." Flora comments. "He's always in his drover clothes. After seeing you in his suit, I'll no want him to remind me of you."

"Flora. Your Allan must be a fine young man."

"He is." Flora has grown attached to the Prince. There is a sadness that they will soon part.

The rain is still lashing down. The Prince has changed into a dry shirt and a philibeg. The plates before them are empty. The three men have been supping heavily on whisky.

Flora sits perched and detached. Sandy enters again, whispers to Donald Roy.

"The rain's no letting up. The MacLeods are fretting to get you to the mainland."

"I would prefer to stay in the inn for the night."

"You will be recognised. You must go with the MacLeods this evening."

The Prince takes out his pipe. "Landlord! Tobacco for the gentleman."

MacNab "Right away, Mister Thompson."

Neil throws a look of concern at his familiarity with the landlord.

"Donald. Are you travelling with me?"

"My foot, Mr. Thomson. I am a cripple and until it heals, I risk losing it with the gangrene."

"I understand. However, I'm wary to leave without a MacDonald with me. Neil?"

"I must make plans for your ship. I cannot do it by hiding with you."

"Of course. Right now I feel safe with you three by me."

Flora is forthright. "Tis the whiskey giving you the comfort."

The Prince sits up. "Flora. You are a gift to womankind."

MacNab lays a chunk of tobacco on the table. The Prince presses him with a sixpence. He goes away.

"The Raasay men are very able, sir"

Donald Roy agrees. "Neil speaks wisely. You'll know them, sir, except Rona. They were at the raising of the Standard, and the march to Derby."

"Captain O'Neil is to join you in Raasay."

The Prince's hopes are raised. "Felix is in Skye?"

Neil "No, he is at Mrs MacKenzie's in Stornoway and hoping to cross soon to Raasay."

The Prince is slowly getting a picture of the plan they have for him. "Then I must trust your trust in the MacLeods." He raises his glass. "I give thanks to all the MacDonalds who have preserved my life." He downs the draught.

Sandy enters, loiters at the door. He signals that the way is safe.

Donald Roy and the Prince rise.

"God speed, sir. I will see Flora safe to her mother's in Armadale."

"Neil, you have borne my uneasy company without complaint. You have been a true friend."

"And you, sir."

Charles presses a small silver cased miniature portrait of himself into Flora's hand.

"Until we meet again, Flora."

He kisses her hand. And with that final gesture, he turns and leaves the inn with Donald Roy.

Flora flops down in reflection and disbelief that her adventure is over. "As my tutor, Neil, you made me read a hundred stories, but I never read one like this."

"You don't need to read this one, Flora, you are in it."

Flora stares down at the miniature, clutches it tightly and sighs.

Rona MacLeod, twenty four, his brother, shoulder wounded Murdoch aged twenty two, and their cousin Captain Malcolm, all of thirty-six, with two MacLeod boatmen who have also served in the Prince's army, wait by their small boat.

Donald Roy leads the Prince to them. Charles sees the boat and baulks.

"I've had my fill of small boats!"

"Please, sir, get in.," pleads Rona.

The Prince gets into the boat.

"Carry him safely, Rona." Donald Roy fades into the gloom.

6

It is midday and they are resting in a shieling on Raasay. The MacLeods are eating simple fare with the Prince who sits apart. The men are more battle worn than the MacDonalds. Malcolm keeps watch at the door.

The Prince is partly hung over, partly melancholic at being left with his new guardians. "How has life been since Culloden?

Murdoch MacLeod "Scott ordered the slaughter of all the animals on Raasay ... then left them to rot."

Rona MacLeod is equally bitter. "They raped a blind girl. Flogged two of our family. One died and the other is crippled for life."

Murdoch adds "They have robbed everyone, stripped them, turned them out, burnt their cottages to the ground.

"Three hundred cottages burnt ... this is one of the few they missed."

The Prince is visibly shocked. "No more please, I beg you. I mean no offence. Better days will return. Surely God does not design these events for no cause?"

"The Jacobite cause." Rona is accusative.

The Prince is uncomfortable at the way he is being spoken to.

"Gently does it," Malcolm is staring out "... the Peddler's back."

Malcolm signals the Prince to come to him. Together they crawl out of the hut on all fours.

A Peddler comes into view. He is an odd sight, his coat made from many patches, originally of the Campbell plaid.

"He's a furtive-faced fellow," the Prince observes.

"Came here to sell tobacco. Narrow slits for eyes and a habit of looking sideways. A spy. Writing dispatches for Cumberland."

Malcolm slowly raises his musket, takes aim.

"He does no harm!"

Rona and Murdoch have crawled out of the shieling and join them in the grass.

Rona "Shoot him dead, Malcolm."

The Prince is insistent. "No, I say. God forgive that we take any poor man's life in saving our own."

Rona. "You may be Prince, but we are the parliament. Fire, Malcolm."

The Peddler suddenly turns in a different direction, moves away from the hut.

"See, he is passing at a safe distance!" The Prince is pleased.

The MacLeods are not pleased with him. They think he is weak.

The Peddler disappears from view.

The MacLeods settle silently back into their positions in the hut. No one speaks. The Prince feels isolated and lonely.

In Kingsburgh House, Lieutenant MacCaghan and two Redcoats follow Kingsburgh and Mrs. Kingsburgh into the room where the Prince has slept.

Captain Ferguson is inspecting the bed.

MacCaghan "The Captain wants to know about your recent lodgers. Please be distinct in your answers."

Mrs. Kingsburgh "If Captain Ferguson is to be my judge, then God have mercy on my soul!"

"Why do you speak of me in such fashion, madam?"

"Your reputation precedes you. You are a very cruel hearted man."

Ferguson is put out, caught short for words. "People should not believe all the world says." He addresses Kingsburgh directly. "Is this where the person along with Miss MacDonald slept?"

"I know which room Miss MacDonald lay herself, but not the servant. My wife will inform you of that."

Ferguson's face twists in malice. "Madam. Did you

lay the Young Pretender and Miss MacDonald in this one bed?"

"Sir! I can assure you that it is not the fashion in the Isle of Skye to lay the mistress and the maid in the same bed!"

"This is the best room in the house. Tis remarkable that the room in which the maid sleeps is better than the one where the mistress has slept???"

The Kingsburghs have no answer.

"Arrest him."

Kingsburgh is seized and bound.

"Donald!"

"Madam. He is a traitor. Consider yourself fortunate that you will not hang with him."

The MacLeod's are sleeping. The Prince is up and packed. He quietly departs. Malcolm stirs.

There is a glorious night sky - the Prince stands and breathes in the air.

Malcolm emerges from the shieling.

"Can you not sleep, your lordship?"

"I'm ready to journey on, MacLeod." He shows him his pack.

"Journey where, your lordship? We are to wait here for Captain O'Neil, then take you to the MacKenzies."

"I am uneasy about remaining here any longer. The tales you have told have alarmed me. I want to go back to Skye."

The Prince walks off at a pace.

Malcolm realises that the Prince is not turning back. He returns to the shieling.

"Rona! Up! We are taking the madman back to Skye."

Rona is only half awake. Malcolm leaves in haste.

Rona and Murdoch rise, gather their arms.

The Prince has had his way. Dawn is coming up and the MacLeods are rowing him back to Skye. They land him on the beach at Scorrybreac.

The Prince leaps out of the boat and begins to scramble up to the raised beach above the shore. The MacLeods watch in disbelief.

The Prince is striding along a coastal path.

Malcolm catches up with him. "You foolish man! You are heading into Portree!"

The Prince stops, turns.

"Now, sir, you cannot go about aimlessly or you will be apprehended within an hour. Where is it that you wish to travel?"

"I hope to put myself in the hands of the McKinnon's."

"Why, sir? We are meant to hand you to the MacKenzies."

"You MacLeods have treated me roughly. I don't believe you have my interests at heart."

"Now, sir, that is hardly the case. We have exposed ourselves to great danger in our assistance to you."

"And myself?"

Malcolm turns conciliatory. "Let's wipe the slate clean, your lordship. If it is the MacKinnon country you wish to get to, I have a sister in MacKinnon country. I am at your service."

The Prince considers his options. His temper has cooled and the reality of being on his own is setting in. "Then MacLeod, I throw myself entirely into your hands. Do with me as you please."

"Gladly. In my mind it is easier to get to MacKinnon country by boat than go cross-country.

"I refuse to get into the boat with those other MacLeods!"

"Then how shall we get there?"

"I intend to walk, and I know the way!"

The Prince turns about, but does not know which way to go.

"Sir! I know the way better than you. It is a long walk ... as much as thirty miles by the direct highway, but we must for safety, use bye ways."

"I am agreed. But I am not walking by night, for if harm befalls me in some foul bog, you will be held responsible!

"You will have your way, sir, but you must pretend to be my servant.

"I'm tired of being servants."

"Then you are doomed to be caught."

The Prince gives into MacLeod's logic of using yet another disguise. "Alas then, Mister MacLeod. How will we pass it off?"

"You will walk a little way behind me and carry the baggage. I'm sure that you've had many a servant in your better days. Just think, as they must. I'm the man of importance, you the wretch of no importance."

"You are a scoundrel, MacLeod."

"We are but playing parts, your lordship. If we are challenged, you refer to me as 'master', and I to you as 'Lewie Caw'?"

"What sort of name is that?

"You are the son of Mr. Caw the Surgeon from Crieff."

The Prince recognises the name. "He was out with us in our late affairs?"

"He was, your lordship."

"What if I were to meet Mr. Lewie Claw himself on this here road?"

"Then it would be his ghost. He died of fever November past."

The Prince is satisfied. "Then I am content to be Lewie Caw."

"I am pleased for it. We will have to negotiate very high hills and traverse wild boggy moors."

"Captain MacLeod. I am a seasoned moor tramper. Have no fear of me being shy of hardship."

Malcolm hands the Prince his baggage and excess arms. "Follow me then, Lewie."

Malcolm strikes across a moor. The Prince trails behind him.

Tis some hours later and they are travelling south towards the Cuillins. The magnificent hills stretch out before Malcolm and the Prince as they traverse a ridge. Behind them can be seen the panorama of the Long Island archipelago were the Prince has spent the two previous months.

They travel high along the hilltop ridges.

"What would you do if we came across a party of soldiers, Lewie?"

"Fight, to be sure."

"If there were no more than four of them, I could do for two."

"I would do for the other two."

"How would you do them?" Malcolm enquired.

"Sword, pistol and knife."

"I prefer my hands, especially Redcoats. Strangle the life out of them."

"Clean, but hardly quick. We would need to do the deed and move swiftly on."

"Aye, the escape is a consideration. Pistol may be the best after all."

They are now in the folds of the high Cuillins. The Prince is very animated. He can't stop talking.

"Back we marched to Culloden House as you now, arriving at six in the morning. I ordered provisions for the men, went into the house, threw myself upon the top of a bed, boots and all."

He takes a breath.

"In a few hours, the enemy arrived. I hurried to the field, drew the men up in two lines, but they were fatigued or dispersed looking for food. I could not get them all together."

They emerge from the trees.

"When the cannonading began, I had less than three thousand men in the field, and not in the best order. I was in the rear ordering men into position. I sent an aid-de-camp with orders to Murray to make the attack. He was killed by cannon shot. I sent off a second and a third aid-de-camp with orders to attack. Still nothing happened."

Malcolm rests in the heather. The Prince continues to talk.

"My left was flanked by a great body of Cumberland's horse and never got up to give their fire."

"I was on the right, sir..."

"The right did well, broke in upon the enemy, sword in hand, Atholl's men, Stewarts, Camerons, and what was left of the MacDonalds did great execution." The Prince is struggling to recall what occurred next.

"Until the grapeshot..."

"Yes, then we were much reduced by grapeshot. Lochiel and Keppoch were carried of. On seeing this, you men lost heart and fled."

"We did not flee. It was a tactical retreat. We saw no purpose to further losses when we saw the battle was lost."

He sighs. "I do not think the battle was lost at that time. But when the left saw you fleeing, they gave way themselves, and turned.

The Prince throws himself into the heather. "I am ashamed to say that it was not my Highlanders but the Low Country men that kept me guarded till I ordered them to fend for themselves."

The Prince is disturbed by Malcolm's silence. "Apart from the odd detail, the battle was over in an hour. Do you think that is a fair assessment?

Malcolm says nothing.

The Prince looks at him. "Have you no comment to make about my leadership?"

Malcolm stands up. He approaches Charles, takes from his baggage a set of bagpipes. He skirls the pipes with some swift movements of his arm.

He plays a pibroch. The music sweeps over the mountains. It is a melancholic tune, a dirge.

Malcolm lowers his pipes.

"Are you yourself again, MacLeod?"

"Aye, I am."

"What was that you played?"

"The Lament for Prince Charles."

Malcolm packs the bagpipes back into his baggage. "We better away. If that doesnae bring the Redcoats upon us, then they are deaf."

"We are on top of the mountains."

"Aye, but they would have been able to hear my pibroch in Portree."

Malcolm sets off. Lewie is made to run after him.

"You are a strange man, Malcolm MacLeod."

"That I am. And you, Lewie Caw, are stranger still."

The heat of the day is on them. The Prince stops, takes a drink from a small stream.

"Lewie! Tis not good for your constitution to drink ice cold water when you are perspiring."

"Not at all, MacLeod, it will not hurt me in the least. If you drink any cold thing when you are warm, remember to piss after drinking."

"To piss?"

"Yes, piss, and it will do you no harm at all! I have this advice from a very good friend abroad."

The Prince uncorks a bottle of brandy – drink to wash down the water.

"You make a fine young doctor, sir, you drink like one."

He snatches the bottle from 'Lewie', swigs heartily.

The Prince is scratching incessantly. Malcolm observes his young companion, and takes pity on him.

"Och, you are an abomination, Lewie. You have the itch. Open the breast of your shirt."

Charles does as he is told and Malcolm inspects his torso. He is covered in bite marks.

"You are lousy, man! Get off with your shirt."

"We are high in the mountains. It is cold."

Malcolm gives him a look. He strips. Malcolm throws the shirt into a ravine. He takes a fresh one from his baggage.

"Now give me your philibeg."

The Prince loosens his belt, unwinds his plaid and offers it to Malcolm. He takes it at an arms length and lays it on an open piece of ground.

"You are a bother, Lewie. Have yourself a wash in yon stream then I'll give you this shirt."

Twenty minutes later, Malcolm having painstakingly cleared the plaid of lice, squeezes the last one in his fingers. "I counted fourscore." He throws Charles his plaid.

Charles, washed and wearing the clean shirt, rewinds his plaid around his hips, and tightens his belt. He is cold. He takes a long swig on the brandy.

"I picked up the itch in the shieling on Raasay."

"No, we MacLeods keep a clean island. We never have the itch." Malcolm takes the bottle from Charles.

Charles smiles. He has finally managed to needle Malcolm.

Loch Slappin lies ahead. To the south on the Ergol peninsula, lies MacKinnon country.

The Prince stops to adjust his cap. "The MacKinnons were with us all the way to Derby and back. They will know me. Will I blacken my face?"

"You might be taken for an African heathen and provoke more curiosity. Take off your wig."

The Prince does as he is told.

Malcolm takes a dirty napkin - ties it around the Prince's head. He places his bonnet back on his head.

The Prince is unhappy. "At least Betty Burke had a clean headscarf."

Malcolm stands back, studies him. "Hmmm?" He is not convinced by the success of the package that is Lewie Caw.

"It is an odd remarkable face I have. Nothing can disguise it."

"Aye, but you could dissemble your air."

"How do you mean?"

"Tis the way you are standing. Dressed as you are, there's something not ordinary, something still of the stately and the grand."

"Its four hundred years of Stuart kingship. How am I to lose that in an instance?"

"Aye, sir, I see that, but can you just try for my sake to be Lewie Caw."

Catherine MacKinnon, a woman of thirty, halts by her door to watch the approach of her brother Malcolm and 'Lewie'.

"Catherine!"

"Malcolm! You are safe from the fighting!"

"I am. And your man? Is he safe home?"

"Aye, God sent him back to me."

"Is he in?"

"He's away on the laird business. He'll be back this night."

"Well, sister, if you don't mind, I've come to bide awhile?"

Catherine gives 'Lewie' a sideways look. "You're aye welcome, Malcolm. Come in. I'll have the lassie make you a wash."

They follow Catherine into the cottage. MacLeod removes his bonnet. He beckons Lewie to do the same.

"This is my servant Lewie. "

The Prince makes a low bow, and sits down a little way off.

"I like him unco well, Malcolm. You've done well to get such a good-looking servant. Where'd you find him?"

"Och, I got him on my travels in England."

"Prince Charlie must have been paying you well?"

"Och aye but I was nae in it for the money."

"Was it the glory then, like MacKinnon?"

"Aye, you could say it was for the glory of going to England and scaring the life out of them. You have no ken of how they live there, Catherine. They have meat every night, and drink beer like its come free from a mountain burn."

Catherine puts some food out on the table.

"Lewie. Come and eat. Don't be shy."

Malcolm throws off his shoes. He signals Lewie to do the same.

Catherine looks closely at how dirty they both are. "Fionna!"

Fionna MacGregor, a young serving girl, pops her head around a door.

In Gaelic "Bring a tub and water." Catherine pours a bowl of water over Malcolm and Lewie's hands. "Have you no been sticking to the highways?"

Fionna runs in with the tub of water.

In Gaelic "Wash the Captain's feet, Fionna."

Fionna bends down begins to wash Malcolm's muddy-caked legs.

In Gaelic "That's a good lass. When you're finished wash my servant's feet as well."

Fionna springs up indignant. In Gaelic "No such thing! I'll wash the master's feet, but I'll no be touching the likes of him!"

Malcolm laughs at the girl.

In Gaelic "Fionna! You can see that Lewie is a quiet gentle soul. Let's show him some hospitality."

Fionna huffs and puffs - bends - lifts the tub - shuffles reluctantly over to Lewie. Malcolm winks at 'Lewie'.

Fionna starts to wash Lewie's legs with a cloth. She goes roughly about her task as she moves up his leg. In a fit of pique, she pushes the cloth right up beyond his thigh and between his legs.

"For the sake of God!" The Prince cries out.

The uttering in English scares the daylights out of Fionna. She takes hold of her tub, runs out as fast as her thin legs can carry her.

Malcolm and Catherine laugh loudly. Lewie tries to raise a smile.

It is late in the day. Malcolm is sitting on a grassy knoll. In the distance, he recognises the tall striding figure of Captain John MacKinnon, his thirty-four year old brother in law.

He rises and goes to greet him. They embrace as comrades, men who have been to war together and survived.

Lewie is playing with the MacKinnon's small five-year-old son. He has him in his arms and is singing to him a Jacobite song.

"You'll be a captain in my service when you grow up." He throws him in the air, catches him.

Malcolm and John enter. John is incredulous at seeing Charles playing with his son.

"Lewie. My brother in law John, a captain in the Prince's service."

Malcolm closes the door for privacy. The introduction is a charade. John knows Lewie to be the Prince.

John sinks slowly to his knees, starts to cry. The Prince bends down and lifts him up.

"We are all battle weary, John. All of us are coming to terms with the loss at Culloden."

"I can bear the loss. The worst is to see you in such straights, sir."

The Prince looks him straight in the eyes. "My looks are deceiving. I am well and healthy and the better for Highland life. MacLeod has taught me some new tricks."

John rises, cheered by the Prince's good nature. "I will take you to the MacKinnon. He will be glad to know you are here."

It is a small dark cottage near the shore of Ergol. The Chief MacKinnon aged seventy-one, embraces the Prince.

"Laddie! You've lost some weight. Have you no been eating your porridge every morning?"

"Alas chief, there have been some mornings when I have not been hungry."

"You're a brave, laddie. Your man Alex MacDonald has been passing through here from time to time. He told us about your wanderings in the Uists. Did you no get any rest?"

"Some, chief. A few sleepless nights."

"Well, you're in the hands of old MacKinnon himself now, and it is my task to get you to the continent. There's Redcoats everywhere." He touches the side of his nose with his forefinger. "We have to be smart, laddie."

"You are the only chief on Skye who came out for me."

"And I'd do it again! I came out for your father in the Fifteen and they took everything from me then. At seventy-one, they'll never break me. I'm a MacKinnon!" He slaps the Prince on the back. "Now, laddie, what are we going to do with you?

"That is my quandary, chief. I am trapped in Scotland until I can find a ship for France."

"Aye, you are, but before long, we'll be having Redcoats and the militia here again looking for you."

"What is your advice?"

"I take you myself to Moidart. The Glenaladale boys are living in the hills. They will be able to hide you in some yon cave."

"May I rest here for the night under your roof?"

"Tis a poor man's bed I'll have for you?"

"I am glad for a bed instead of a rock or a cow shed."

"As an old soldier, I ken your feeling, laddie." MacKinnon puts his hand on the Prince's shoulder. "Tonight you'll rest. In the morning you'll have a grand breakfast. Leave everything else to me."

The MacKinnons have loaded a boat and it sits on the water with four oarsmen. There is a small gathering of the clan on the shoreline. The Chief is giving his farewells to his kin, John to his wife and his son.

The Prince hands Malcolm a letter. "My apologies to your MacLeod cousins for my ill humour. And Donald Roy. Make my thanks to all those whom I have given such trouble."

The Prince pushes a silver buckle and ten guineas into Malcolm's hand.

"Lewie. I have only done my duty."

"No arguments, please. I'm tired of our bickering." The Prince puts his cutty pipe into his mouth. "I am Lewie no more. Light me up, MacLeod. Let us share a last pipe together."

Malcolm smiles, puts a piece of tow to the pan of his pistol - snaps it - puts the tow to the pipe. The Prince lights up, takes a draw, and then hands the pipe to Malcolm.

"Remember me every time you suck on it." He shakes Malcolm's hand, and Malcolm warmly returns the shake.

"And me every time you itch, your lordship."

The Prince laughs.

Malcolm and the clan gathering step forward on the rocky shoreline to watch as the Prince sails with Old MacKinnon and Captain John out into the waters of Loch Scavaig.

They watch until all that is left in their vision are the isles of Soay, Canna and Rhum. They run and climb the steep slope to the village and from the high cliffs train their eyes on the tiny speck until it disappears into the Sound.

The day is the 5th July. The MacKinnon boat is off the Knoydart peninsula. The Prince is lying on the boards covered with a plaid. He pops his head up.

"Where are we?"

John MacKinnon pushes him down. "Loch Nevis!"

From shoreward, a boat with five Militiamen is rowing towards them.

"Ready your muskets, laddies."

The old Chief is ready for a fight. The men ship their oars and start priming their rifles.

"Wait for my order..."

The Prince pops up again "There's to be no bloodshed, MacKinnon."

"Aye, lad, I agree, but if they open fire we are obliged to return volley."

The Prince snatches a quick look at the militia boat. "That's an unworthy boat they have. Can we not outrun them?"

John considers the idea. "There's a good chance."

Old MacKinnon looks at the Prince, taps the side of his nose. "You're a smart, laddie. Lay your arms, MacKinnons. Full sail and row with all your might."

They men take to the oars.

They cross the path of the militiamen. They militiamen fire on them, but their shots fall short. The MacKinnon boat pulls away, and within ten minutes, the militia boat is seen to give up any attempt at pursuit.

They land on a sandy beach in Knoydart near the end of Loch Nevis. They disembark. After their provisions have been unloaded, John MacKinnon sends the boatmen away.

The Prince, John and the Chief are alone. There is the smell of burning in the air. Across the loch, a plume of smoke rises. The Chief is resigned to what is happening.

"The Redcoats are burning every house from here to Lochaber. Same as in the Fifteen."

"Have we no friends left in Knoydart?

"Everyone of our cause is lost at Culloden, imprisoned, or fled. We must do for ourselves and proceed by foot to Borrodale. You still have loyal friends there.

"Mr. MacKinnon. It is fifty miles or more to Borrodale. You are three score and ten."

"I can endure hardship better than most young men. Let us proceed by way of Morar."

They take a well-worn track and have not travelled far, when by chance they come upon a large baronial house with gardens. The house is still intact; there is no sign of pillage or destruction.

"Tarbet House. Tis owned by Clanranald." Old MacKinnon speaks his name with vitriol. "He rents it to one of the Glengarry MacDonalds."

"Then it should be marked for reprisals." John adds.

The Prince is puzzled. "Could it be that the Redcoats have not discovered it?"

MacKinnon is dismissive. "Tis a well known house. It has not been forgotten, it has been spared as Clanranald did not come out for you."

The Prince "Shall we call?"

MacKinnon is adamant "We will not. We will go round by the water and hurry past.

They are executing their plan, when a chance glance by the Prince, spots a lone figure in the gardens. Charles halts the others, makes them crouch and observe from behind cover.

"Its the old fox himself. Clanranald."

Chief MacDonald is exercising his swordsmanship. He is stiff and ungainly."

"He is hardly battle trained" MacKinnon scoffs.

"Shall we approach him?"

"Och, you leave this to me. I have many a score to

settle with that man."

The MacDonald is out of breath from his exertions.

MacKinnon, older but lighter on his feet, stalks Clanranald as he gathers his plaid. Then out of the corner of his eye, MacDonald catches sight of MacKinnon, and in fright, scurries away towards the house. MacKinnon catches him by his coattail.

"Oh Mr MacKinnon, it is you? How do you do? It's not easy to know the people who come visiting these days. I took you for an enemy."

"I've come with orders for you."

"No, I am too old for this. I will lose everything! Is he here? I know he is here!" MacDonald is looking about frantically for the Prince. "He cannot come into the house! The army will be back to raze and burn and rob us of everything!"

"You did not come out in the Fifteen for the father, and again you have not come out for the son."

"I tell you, MacKinnon, I know no-one in whose hands I can put him. My family has been ruined! Ruined I say! My wife and brother have been put in goal, my household turned upside down and ransacked. Donald Campbell, Donald MacLeod, his son, my boatmen, ... anyone who has aided him has been arrested and interrogated by the Redcoats!"

"Then you will know what I suffered after the Fifteen, and like many others, suffer again."

"He had no right to come and make his old father's claim for the crown! Look what has happened to my sons and followers? Hunted through the glens, their houses burnt, their cattle slaughtered, their wives and children turned out naked! For what? A pipe dream for one foreign wee laddie to put his father above us all in London!"

"You are a toady, MacDonald. The Prince is less foreign than the fat German you have adopted as your master. You are a fool."

"No, you are the fool, MacKinnon! I was never for such a naive venture. To invade England! It had failure written large across it. My entire family were against me, but I have been proven right. It's a death sentence now for any one caught aiding him. My advice is that you should return directly to Skye and land him on Raasay. Leave him with those renegade MacLeod's long enough, and he'll surrender himself."

MacKinnon is in a fury. "Raasay has been burnt and plundered. In the name of King George. Not a goat or sheep can hide there. Was it always your plan to throw the Prince directly into the hands of our enemies?"

Two MacDonald retainers come out of the house, their muskets raised. MacKinnon backs off.

"MacDonald has upheld its honour. Tis MacKinnon, MacLeod and Cameron business now!"

MacKinnon draws his pistol. "I'd shoot you dead, but I'll no hang for killing a coward."

"Get off my land, MacKinnon, or I'll have my men shoot you as by the law for being a renegade!"

"If that be the best advice you can give, MacDonald, you better keep it to yourself or we MacKinnons, MacLeods and Camerons in one great horde will be back here to kill, burn and plunder your lands better than Cumberland's whole army!"

MacKinnon back steps until he feels it is safe to turn, and slip away.

Some hours have passed. The Prince and the MacKinnons are travelling the loch side road that runs the length of Morar. They have been in hot conversation for most of the way.

MacKinnon "He is a raving madman and a danger to you."

"Well, I thank MacDonald and his family well enough for their aide on the Long Island."

At length, they come to the end of the loch where the river Morar cuts deep across a short piece of land little more than a quarter of mile wide, tumbles over a waterfall, and then out into the sea.

The river crossing is dangerous, and it is custom to have assistance in crossing. Nearby, a Fordman sits in a small shelter, waiting for custom.

Captain MacKinnon in Gaelic "You there! Will you carry this poor fellow across on your back?"

He is pointing to the Prince.

The Fordman is indignant. "The devil be on my back if I carry any servant like him. I only carry gentlemen!"

He points to the old MacKinnon.

"I'll take you if you please, old sir."

Old MacKinnon looks at the river, turns his back on the Fordman. "The devil with him. If you must wade, then I will wade with you and save a penny."

Charles takes s a coin from his purse. "On my account, please avail yourself of the Fordman."

"Och no, tis a waste to encourage a man to be idle but for a few minutes every day, just for a penny. Tis time they put a bridge over this water."

MacKinnon hikes up his kilt. "Give me your arm, man."

All three cross the river arm in arm.

The Prince is curious. "What is it with these Highland servants? They are right haughty?"

"Och, they have an over inflated sense of worth. One minute heroic in self-denial, the next, full of grand self-importance. They are a devil to govern!"

Aboard the Furness, Captain Ferguson is with General Campbell in the ship's cabin. It is a Spartan interior as Ferguson is not the type of man who indulges in material comfort. As a native of Old Meldrum, his schooling and religious education have made him frugal and mean.

Flora is ushered in.

"Miss Macdonald." Ferguson approaches Flora with evil intent.

General Campbell is getting to know the man and pre-empt him. "Captain Ferguson! Lay one finger on that lady, and I will have you shot!"

"On what grounds, General?"

"I don't need grounds, Ferguson. I'm your commanding officer."

Campbell gets up, offers his chair to Flora. "Please make yourself comfortable, Miss MacDonald?"

Meanwhile MacCaghan shows Ferguson the miniature portrait of the Prince that he has confiscated from Flora. Ferguson smiles, turns to his question his pretty prisoner.

"Miss MacDonald. What were the movements of the Young Pretender after he left you?"

"I do not know. From Portree, I went to my mother's in Armadale where I heard you wished to see me."

"So you don't deny that you were with the Young Pretender."

"Sir. The person you refer to as the Young Pretender? Are you referring to Charles Edward Stuart?"

"Don't be impertinent with me! Do you know that I could have you flogged?"

"Ferguson! You will refrain from threatening Miss MacDonald."

"General! I am trying to conduct an enquiry here!"

"You will behave in accordance with judicial law!"

"Sir, we are aboard a ship and thus under maritime law?"

"Do not push your favour with me, Ferguson. Do not be afraid of him. Miss MacDonald."

"I am not afraid, sir. Captain Ferguson is doing his duty as an officer of the King. On the other hand, I have done my duty as a Highland lass. I have given charity when it was needed, and assistance when it was asked."

"And from all accounts, with great courage, Miss MacDonald. That will be all, thank you."

"This is poppycock!"

Campbell ignores Ferguson and addresses MacCaghan. "Lieutenant. Confine Miss MacDonald with the other members of her family."

"General, I protest! I have not finished questioning her!"

"Follow my orders, MacCaghan."

"Yes, sir." MacCaghan smiles. He is enjoying the spectacle of Ferguson being out-ranked.

MacCaghan hands Flora her miniature, and takes her out.

Flora is put into confinement in a crowded hold. Rory, John MacDonald, and their Boatmen, make room for her. Behind them, cramped in a small-seated area are Lady Clanranald, Kingsburgh, Donald MacLeod, Young Donald, Donald Campbell, Malcolm MacLeod, and Felix O'Neil. Lady Clanranald is in a state of nervous breakdown. O'Neil is comforting her.

O'Neil brightens. "Flora! I knew I'd see you again."

The Kingsburghs take her by the hands.

"Are we all taken?"

O'Neil lowers his voice. "Not on your life. Alex MacLeod, Ned, your cousin Neil..."

Flora likewise speaks softly. "The Prince?"

Malcolm whispers. "The Prince has crossed to Knoydart."

"May God protect him."

There is a mutter of "Amen."

The Prince and his companions rest by an old Celtic Cross. A church before them is burnt out and is still smouldering, evidence of the plunder and ruin being perpetrated by the Redcoats.

"Tis the work of the devil." The old chief looks skywards, "Lord, is it our punishment to be born in such times?"

Captain John puts his hand on his uncle's shoulder to comfort him.

The Prince is down on one knee praying. He crosses

himself, and then rises.

They gather themselves, and travel on.

By the end of day, the party of three come upon a bothy. There is no sign of life other than the smoke coming out of the thatch.

Captain John breaks into the bothy, pistol in hand. Allan Roy MacDonald of Morar faces him with a claymore in his hand.

"MacKinnon!"

"Morar!" John lowers his pistol. "We thought you dead?"

"Burnt out, John, burnt out." He is highly distressed. In the corner there is movement. John lights a candle and progresses into the corner of the bothy. Crouched in the corner is Marjory Cameron, his wife, and her two small children.

"Jesus save us. Is that you Marjory? Come." He offers his hand. "Tis John from Ergol."

John helps Catherine and her two children into the light. It is obvious from Catherine's clothing that she has been violated. "Redcoats?"

She nods. She is ashamed to admit it.

"It was Ferguson's men. They came by boat."

"Come..." John leads everyone out of the bothy and into the warm of the summer evening. He sits Catherine on a bench and then shouts "Tis clear!"

The Prince and Chief MacKinnon appear in the clearing before the bothy. The Prince is shocked at the scene before him. Old MacKinnon has been through the Fifteen.

"Marjory Cameron! Tis a fine sight to see you looking so braw. I'd marry you in an instant if it wasnae for Morar here."

Marjory smoothes her hair and rises to greet the old man. "John MacKinnon. You don't look a day older than when you attended my wedding near ten years ago."

"Naw, but I feel it. And how are you young

Marjory?"

Marjory raises half a smile. "I'm fine, Laird John, just fine."

"Well, everything's grand then. I'll be expecting some supper for myself and my companions." He steps into the doorway of the bothy. "Well, it's a grand house you have. It's bigger than mine!" He goes inside.

Marjory takes charge "Away children, fetch the water. Come, inside, gentlemen."

The Prince is gracious "After you, Mrs. MacDonald." Marjory goes in goes inside.

The Prince takes MacDonald by the arm. "She is Donald and Archie Cameron's sister?"

Morar is also ashamed. "T'was the reason the Redcoats took her after burning our house. I found her naked hiding in a cave."

As the bothy contains no furniture, they are squatting on the earthen floor. Marjory removes a blackened pot from an open fire as supper for her guests. Unaware of the Prince's true identity, as Marjory ladles a meagre measure to fill the Prince's plate, he rests his hand on hers. She looks at him.

"Do you not know who I am, Miss Cameron? You visited me many years ago in Paris with your brother Lochiel."

Marjory's eyes slowly rise up and look straight into the Prince's.

"God save us! It's the Prince!" Morar throws himself back from the table. "I cannot give you shelter! I am such danger. I have my family to think of."

The two young children rush and cower in the corner. Marjory Cameron puts down her serving pot.

"You are a coward, husband. Pull yourself together! Tis his highness you are speaking to!"

The Prince appeals to Morar. "We have not eaten since yesterday. We are in want of food."

"Then you will have more than these potatoes! I

have some cold salmon that my worthless husband has hidden from you."

The Prince gets up. He is shaking. "Miss Cameron. I have brought this woe on you all with my campaigning!"

"I will not hear it! What is done is done. Come, sit...."

The Prince resettles on the floor.

Marjory and Morar go out. They can be heard arguing.

"He has not provided us with the full story." John MacKinnon states.

They try not to listen to the arguing in Gaelic going on outside. Old MacKinnon collects the children into his arms.

John relates. "He deserted her when the Redcoats came."

The Prince nods. "I pray you would not desert me if the Redcoats came."

Old MacKinnon is unequivocal. "With the help of god, I will go through the wide world with you to meet our Maker."

Marjory re-enters the hut carrying a gutted salmon.

She cuts up the fish. "Once you have eaten, my husband will take you to Borrodale. The Laird can stay here with us, and rest."

Marjory is holding back her tears. "Please forgive my appearance..."

She begins to sob as she cuts the fish. The three men are at a loss.

Morar leads the Prince and John MacKinnon down a steep slope and through some trees.

"This is not the way to Borrodale House." MacKinnon retorts.

"Borrodale is has been lodging in a bothy as he is a wanted man."

They come upon a thatched dwelling in the woods.

MacKinnon stays the Prince and Morar and approaches the bothy.

He calls in Gaelic. "Friends! Are there any MacDonalds lodged here?"

Angus MacDonald, sixty-five, laird of Borrodale, opens the door with a blanket wrapped around his shoulders.

"Young John!"

"Angus." They exchange hands. "I've come to ask if you have news of the Prince."

"I have nothing. The last I heard he had escaped from Uist."

"What would you give for sight of him?"

"I'd drink a hearty bottle to see him safe." Borrodale realises that MacKinnon has been testing him. "Is he here?"

Borrodale waves his to someone inside who emerges with a pistol in his hand. It is his son Ranald, Young Borrodale, a twenty eight year old who has been covering him.

Captain MacKinnon looks at the young man. "Tis Young Borrodale?"

"Aye, it is" he replies.

"We all had you for dead. Shot by Captain Scott."

"That was my brother John."

"T'was a loss, but we were glad for his boat to Skye." The Prince steps out from the side of the bothy.

Borrodale throws his blanket from his shoulders. "I am mighty pleased! Mighty pleased!" He shakes the Prince's hand vigorously. "How did you find me?"

Morar slinks into view. Young Borrodale seizes his dirk and launches at him. He overwhelms him and pushes him to the ground. He raises his dirk.

MacKinnon pulls him off.

"Get this coward out of my sight! He is a disgrace of a man!"

Morar is quickly up on his feet. "I'm glad to be away!" He turns and speeds off.

MacKinnon "I commit the Prince to your charge, Angus. I have done my duty, do you yours. Farewell, your highness."

John MacKinnon chases after Morar. "Morar! Hold up. I will accompany you home!" Morar stops and allows MacKinnon to catch up with him. Together they disappear into the woods.

Borrodale admits The Prince into his bothy.

Some days have passed and the Prince has been taken into the high hills and made to wait in a small cave above a precipice.

The Prince is gazing out of a cave and puffing on his clay pipe and is reading a book in Italian.

"What are you reading, Charlie?" asks Borrodale.

"Vita de Opapa Sisto V. The Life of Pope Sixtus the Fifth."

"Ranald reads Latin. He studied at the Scots College in Regensburg. Your studies cost me a lot of money, Ranald."

"Aye, father, but I got to travel the Alps. They're no as bonny as these."

"Aye, but they're big?"

"Aye, they're big, but that doesnae mean they're bonny."

"Och you're starting to talk like that adventurer Donald McBane."

From above there is a cry.

"Its Alistair and John!" Borrodale turns to the Prince. The Prince eagerly closes his book.

Major Alistair MacDonald of Glenaladale, thirty-six, and his brother Captain John MacDonald of Glenaladale, thirty-four, approach the cave with haste.

"I came as quick as I could, uncle. Your highness." He gives a small curtsey. His shoulder is patched from grapeshot at Culloden.

"Alistair. I am glad to set eyes on you." The Prince shakes his hand heartily.

They settle.

"I have fresh funds for your keep, sir." He pulls out a heavy purse of coin. "From Donald Cameron."

"Hold it for me, Alistair."

Glenaladale returns the purse to his belt.

Glenaladale sits. "Old MacKinnon was taken yesterday and carried aboard Ferguson's ship."

"Then we must fear the worst for old MacKinnon." Charles has grown accustomed to everyone who helps him being seized after his departure from them. "How close lies the enemy now?"

Glenaladale "We are informed that the fat man has gone back to London. General Campbell's now in charge. He's put he 6th Foot in the front line."

The Prince is recalls Lochboisdale. "Our old enemy, Captain Scott...."

John Glenaladale spreads out a map.

"Campbell's ships of war and tenders are here, here and here. Scott's men have been put ashore at Loch Nevis and Arisaig. He has camps and sentries posted all over the backcountry. They have us trapped in Moidart.

Glenaladale "There are two French ships come for you, anchored off north of the cordon at Poolewe, but there's no chance of us getting you there."

They look to the Prince for instruction. He has none. He is lost in thought.

Glenaladale "John. See uncle Angus home, then go back to Glenfinnan, leave word that we have the Prince, and pass it on to Donald Cameron. We'll meet you on the top of Sgurr a Coireachan."

John Glenaladale folds up his map.

Glenaladale addresses Young Borrodale. "Ronnie, you're coming with us. We're going to need your legs."

The Prince and Glenaladale are climbing to the top of the mountain. Young Borrodale comes bounding back down towards them.

"Redcoats. Coming this way!"

"How many, Ronnie?"

"Five, maybe six hundred?"

"Good god! Go home and tell John to meet us at Doctor Cameron's."

"Aye, sir."

Young Borrodale bounds off down the mountain.

Glenaladale and the Prince traverse sideways.

The Prince and Glenaladale have taken refuge atop a large rock. Below them, spread out, searching the heather are the Redcoats led by Scott.

Scott is taking shade under the rock. The Quartermaster approaches him.

"Can I give the men a rest, sir?"

"No, sergeant. I want this entire hillside searched."

"The men are thirsty, sir?"

"Have them drink the stream water."

"There's a dead sheep in it, sir?"

"Have you ever drunk London water, sergeant?"

"I have not had the pleasure to visit London, sir."

"Even with a sheep in it, that water is better."

"Yes, sir."

The Quartermaster rasps out some orders.

Above on the rock, the Prince is fatigued from remaining motionless. He moves slightly, dislodges some earth.

A pebble drops in front of Scott, and bounces away.

His eyes narrow. He steps out, looks up.

He draws his pistol.

"Captain Scott!"

Scott turns in the direction of the Quartermaster.

"The Young Pretender!"

He points. In the distance, well out of gunshot

range, is Young Borrodale. He has seen the Redcoats, and turned.

The Redcoats to a man give chase.

Scott runs after his men.

On top of the rock the Prince and Glenaladale watch.

"Young Ronnie looks like you from a distance. He'll lead them a dance. He's got the legs of a stag."

The Prince turns over on his back and lets out a sigh of relief. He is exhausted.

"Let's catch some sleep, Charlie."

"I cannot sleep, Alistair. Three months a fugitive. I am fearful that if I close my eyes I will be taken."

Glenaladale throws his plaid over the Prince.

"Sleep. I will be your eyes. Sleep."

Charles slowly closes his eyes... while Glenaladale remains watchful.

It is late evening. Glenaladale is leading the Prince through the heather.

In the near distance is a campsite fire. Glenaladale and the Prince throw themselves into the heather.

"John's right about the militia in the back country."

Out of the gloaming, two men are moving swiftly towards them.

Glenaladale levels his pistol. "Step no further, or I will shoot you dead!"

"Its Ronnie, Alistair. I've brought a friend."

"Have you the Prince?"

The Prince instantly recognises the voice.

"Archie!

"Your highness!" It is Doctor Cameron.

Glenaladale lowers his pistol. Donald takes the Prince's hand, shakes it vigorously.

"How did you find us?"

"Young Borrodale came for me. You're just two miles from my house. The rest was instinct."

"Then it is good fortune. You have my gold?"

Cameron looks perplexed. "If it can be found. It was buried in the dark."

Glenaladale is sceptical. "You made no marker?"

"We were being pursued by the enemy. Our lives were in danger."

Glenaladale cocks his pistol at Cameron. "Tis a tall tale..."

"Let him be, Alistair. We need the doctor's services."

Glenaladale reluctantly lowers his pistol.

"You have need of me, Alistair." Cameron is eying his seeping wound.

"Only a doctor with a Midas touch." Glenaladale is reluctant to have Archie touch him.

"Come along, man. Do you want to live or die?"

As the doctor tends Glenaladale's wounds, the Prince is looking over the brow of the hill with Young Borrodale. Below them is a tented militia encampment. Its men are laughing and joking.

"Campbell Militia?

"Aye. They searched up here yesterday. They'll be gone in the morning.

The Prince settles into the heather, relaxes a little.

John Glenaladale jumps into the hollow. The Prince jumps up with a start.

"You were easy to find."

"Then why have the militia not found me?

"They don't want to find you. The militia are paying lip service to the government.

He pulls two cheeses from his plaid.

"Scott's men are another matter. There's a hundred climbing the other side of the mountain."

They hungrily devour the two cheeses, and then

John leads them away in single file.

Campfires are burning all across the hills. The party of five are moving briskly in the half moonlight.

Suddenly, ahead, a campfire burns brightly. Shadowy figures are laughing and joking loudly.

They pass them by quietly.

Soon, the fires of another camp burn brightly below.

The party makes a detour. It is steep country. The Prince slips and stumbles. His foot goes over a precipice. Glenaladale and Cameron grab him, and pull him back. A few rocks clatter to the bottom below.

The danger has passed. They travel on silently.

It is daylight. Two sentries are patrolling a section of the glen. The party take their chance and pass between them in turns. They are pleased with themselves. They have broken through the cordon.

They slap each other on the back - move on.

It is now the 21st July and they have left the wild mountains of Morar behind, and dropped into Glen Shiel in Lochaber.

The party is lying in the heather, resting. Below on the loch shore, is a detachment of Redcoats. Doctor Cameron and the Prince are watching them conduct their search whilst smoking their pipes.

"How would you feel, your highness, if you were from Warwickshire? Plagued by midges, and wading through peat and bog all day long? You'd want the day to be over." He takes a puff on his pipe. "Every day they wake up and hope that this will be the day they capture the Young Pretender."

"Is that what they call me?"

"Aye, I'm afraid it is."

"Tis an accurate description I would say. However, there's no pretence about my situation."

"No, but its giving every Highlander hope."

"What do you mean?"

"Do you not see? With your get away, we live to fight another day. Culloden is just another battle, not the final one. "

The Prince goes silent.

"Have I offended your highness?"

"No, not at all, Archie. I had no notion of the expectation that is upon me. I thought I had failed you all."

"You haven't failed us, your highness, you have given us Highlanders a voice. The glories of Edinburgh, Carlisle and Manchester. The victories of Prestonpans and Falkirk. You gave us the joy of marching to within a hundred miles of London."

"I miscalculated the mood of the English. I thought they would rise up against the injustices of Whig parliament and Hanover."

"They didn't rise up, no, but they didn't oppose you?"

Glenaladale disturbs them "The Redcoats are moving off."

Doctor Cameron is cheered. "See, they're not interested in finding you. They hate Cumberland and his officers. Forty of Scott's own men deserted to us before Culloden. I'd like to listen at their camp fires to discover their true colours."

The party is crouched in a small pass at the head of Glen Shiel. Below is the road that runs one way to Skye, and the other to Fort Augustus. Two Redcoat sentries are ahead - one to the left, the other to the right.

The Prince jests with Cameron "You want to get closer to hear what they are saying?"

"Tis close enough for me."

They slip past by the sentries one by one and come up on the side of the road and shelter near a farm.

John Glenaladale and Young Borrodale return with a

stone of cheese and a half stone of butter. With them is a boy called McGrath carrying a quart of goat's milk.

The boy looks very shifty. He is taking a good look at the Prince.

Doctor Cameron speaks to him in Gaelic. "Don't be frightened, son. What's your name?"

"McGarth."

"Do you have a first name?" He shakes his head.

"He's a queer boy."

Glenaladale takes out his purse, gives the boy a small coin.

He eyes the purse as Glenaladale closes it again.

Captain Glenaladale dismisses him. "Run along now, son. Not a word to anyone." The boy runs off.

In the other direction, a little distance off, a highlander Donald MacDonald is racing through the heather, looking over his shoulder.

Every twenty strides, he throws himself into the vegetation.

Glenaladale "Do you know him, Cameron? "

"I do. He's a Glengarry man. He marched with us to Derby."

Archie gets up and goes in the direction of the fugitive. He returns with him.

"Donald MacDonald of Glengarry, at your service, major sir!"

"Are you on the run?

"Aye, Scott's men killed my father yesterday. This morning they chased me into the glen."

"Is it possible to get through to Glen Morrison?"

"If you have the right man to guide you."

"Would that be you?"

"Aye, it would." Donald takes a long look at the Prince. He is undecided in his conclusion. "Is that.... naw, he wouldnae be. Is it ... naw, he's just a Highlander.

The Prince grins at him.

"Nae Highlander has teeth like that. Help me God...." He gets down on his knees. "Your royal highness...."

Glenaladale "Get up on your feet, soldier!"

"Aye, major sir. Right away! At your service, sir. Glen Morrison it is."

"You won't need me now. I'll away back home, and gather news." Cameron says meekly.

Glenaladale "You move very freely, Cameron."

"'Tis the privilege of being a doctor at a time when so many are afflicted by the troubles."

He shakes each man by the hand, the Prince last.

"Find the gold, Archie." the Prince smiles.

"Aye, your majesty. I meant to say something about that some days ago but Glenaladale's pistol made me hold my tongue."

Glenaladale turns on Cameron. "Speak up now, you rogue!"

"Well, the truth is, the gold has been dug up and stolen."

"What?" Glenaladale is livid.

"I think it was by Cluny MacPherson."

Glenaladale grabs Cameron by the lapels. "You think it was MacPherson! Another rogue! If you have stolen that gold I will hang you personally!"

The Prince intercedes. "We will have no mischief done to friend or foe. Let Archie be, Alistair."

Glenaladale releases Cameron in disgust. Archie shakes himself down, hands the Prince the last of his tobacco.

"Just remember to keep your pipe lit, your highness, Its a bother to get it going again in the rain." With a broad smile on his face, Cameron turns for home.

Glenaladale is still angry. He signals the party to move off.

Donald MacDonald leads in single file Major Glenaladale, Captain Glenaladale, and the Prince. Young Borrodale brings up the rear. The midges are bad and the Prince has covered his head with his plaid to keep them off.

Gunshots are heard in the distance. They stop and listen. More gunshots.

Glenaladale "Keep moving."

They continue in single file.

It is raining heavily. Glenaladale, the Prince, Young Borrodale are sheltering in an open cave.

They are all wet and miserable.

They watch as Captain Glenaladale and Donald return accompanied by eight well-armed men.

Captain Glenaladale introduces the new member of their party.

"Sir, your new bodyguard. The Seven Men of Glenmorrison"

They introduce themselves in Gaelic.

John MacDonald. Alexander MacDonald. Alexander Chisholm. Donald Chisholm. Hugh Chisholm. Gregor MacGregor. Hugh MacMillan.

The last man, Patrick Grant speaks in English "Sir. We fought under Glengarry's banner at Culloden. The families of Glenmorrison have been hounded from their homes, murdered, tortured. We have vowed to live as outlaws, to steal from the enemy, and give what help we can to our own folk."

"There are eight of you? Yet you call yourself the seven?" asks the Prince.

"That's' to confuse the enemy." Someone translates and the rest laugh.

"Grant is the only one who speaks English. MacDonald however would like to say something on behalf of the men."

The Prince nods.

MacDonald in Gaelic. "It is our sworn oath to

continue hostilities to Cumberland and his army. Our backs are to God and our faces to the Devil. May all the curses that the Scriptures do pronounce might come upon us and all our posterity, if we do not stand firm to help the Prince in his greatest dangers!"

Patrick Grant sums it up. "The Glenmorrison Men are ready to die for you."

The Prince is immediately cheered. "Gentleman I have much to fear, arduous days, and hunger, but not betrayal. I thank you!"

Grant translates. The men are pleased.

Strathglass, 13th August. They are camped in cave under a rocky crag with a small stream nearby. The Glen Morrison men are good foragers. There is ample mutton, deer, butter, and cheese. They are eating well, for time to time with money from the Prince, they send one of their number into Fort Augustus to the merchant kin.

The Prince, in good spirit, has gone native - barefoot, old black kilt coat, philibeg, waistcoat, dirty shirt, long red beard with a musket slung under his arm and a dirk by his side. "We have been here three weeks, Alistair. What I would give for some bread."

"Aye, Charlie. Have you heard what the Glen Morison men now call you?"

"Pray tell. I am curious."

"Dugald MacCullony."

"Dugald MacCullony? What does it mean in Erse, Alistair?"

"Son of the servant of our King?"

"Am I to take the name seriously?"

"No, Charlie, I think it is joke."

"Dugald MacCullony" The Prince repeats it over and over. "Well, I have been given some strange names. MacCullony is the strangest."

"Perhaps tis because you like to cook for the men."

"Ah. I'm their servant?" The Prince smiles. "I have had much practice in Scotland. Perhaps this is the fate of all men of ambition in this country. They come to rule, and learn to serve."

"Aye, that would be a fair notion."

Alexander and Donald Chisholm come racing up the hillside. They speak with Patrick Grant and Young Borrodale, who approach the Prince and the Major.

"Two French officers have been put ashore to find the Prince."

The Prince is elated. "Where are they now?"

"They are in Badenoch."

The Prince is immediately disappointed. That is some fifty miles of more on the other side of the Great Glen.

Major Glenaladale "Get the map, John. The Great Glen is swarming with the enemy, but I'm for breaking through to Badenoch"

They look to the Prince.

"Are you willing to risk it, Charlie?"

For a moment the Prince seems to have settled for a life in the cave. He has forgotten who he is. He studies the men who have struck with him despite the danger and the destruction to their way of life. He has an obligation to free them from his service.

"Gentlemen, I greatly admire your company, but I do not wish to spend winter here. The object is to get me to France. Then if we have to cross the Great Glen, we must. I'm ready to fight if required."

The rest of the men cheer. It is same rousing fighting talk that had led them to Derby. He was still their Prince.

"Give the order, John. We leave at dawn."

Glenaladale clasps the Prince by the shoulder in approval.

The party of thirteen are marching into Glen Garry. The river is swollen and they cannot cross it.

There is distant smoke.

The whole country is still on fire.

They have to sit and wait it out for the river level to drop. It is raining heavily.

They spend a wretched day hiding in a wood.

A detachment of Redcoats travels along a nearby track.

The men have nothing to eat.

The Prince is restless. "Can't we cross further down?

Glenaladale "Its not safe. The bridge is on the road

between Fort Augustus and Fort William. There are at least half a dozen Redcoats are any one time in the guardhouse.

"I'll be the judge of that." The Prince rises to make a start.

Glenmorrison MacDonald in Gaelic. "We'll tie Dugald MacCullony up if he moves one foot!"

"What did he say?

Glenaladale signals to Glenmorrison men that they need not worry.

"It is best to wait, Charlie. They know these roads better than any of us."

The river has been crossed and the party is travelling down the Great Glen towards Loch Lochy. They are in single file and hidden in trees that line the valley. There is deathly silence. There are burnt out cottages, huts, and bothies along the length of the glen. The fields are devoid of cattle, carts or ploughs. Entire hamlets are eerily deserted.

They move into the wood of Kilfillan that runs part way down the north side of Loch Lochy. Wade's military road is on the other side of the loch and the Prince's party see numerous squads of infantry and militia travelling along the road in both directions.

In the safety of the woods, Alexander Chisholm has his musket raised. He fires - brings down a stag.

The majority of the Prince's party have their eyes on the military road on the other side of the loch. A few soldiers have momentarily stopped on the road to consider where the shot has rung out. Their curiosity soon wanes.

Donald and Hugh Chisholm quickly gather the carcass, and carry it between them as the party travels on in single file.

It is night and the deer has been cooked over a large blazing campfire. The Prince is devouring his share of the meat.

"Kings and Princes must be ruled by their privy council. There is not in all the world a more absolute privy council than I have at present." He is high-spirits.

Grant translates his words for the Glenmorrison men. They laugh, and Charles hears the mention of the name 'Dugald MacCullony'.

"And Dugald MacCullony thanks you!" he shouts to them in good humour. They now know he is in on the mockery and they laugh with the Prince.

"When I return will I reward you all. Every last one of you."

Patrick Grant "I recall sir that your great uncle Charles the Second was no so good at keeping his promises to us Highlanders. Nor your own father."

"Tis the ways of the past. I keep my promises. I will be back, you will see by and by."

The Prince's party is now deep in Cameron country. As prearranged by letters carried by the Glenmorrison men, Doctor Cameron and his Cameron cousin Lochgarry are waiting for the Prince at the waterfall that tumbles out of Loch Arkaig. The Prince approaches Cameron accompanied by Glenaladale.

"Where is the Prince?" Doctor Cameron is looking beyond to the Glenmorrison men standing guard a little way off.

"Dugald MacCullony at your service, Archie."

Cameron looks at the sight before him. Dugald removes his bonnet. Cameron is shocked

"Your highness? What has befallen you? Have these outlaws been abusing you?"

"No, not at all. Not at all. I have had most excellent company. I am in excellent health."

Glenaladale is to the point. "Have our Frenchmen been found?"

"They are captured and taken to Ferguson."

"And the French ships?" asks the Prince.

"Departed."

The Prince is visibly deflated by the news.

"I have instructions from Lochiel to proceed immediately to him."

"Where is he?"

"At Cluny's Cage."

"With MacPherson???" Glenaladale turns to Charles. "They are all getting rich at your expense, Charlie. Look at their clothes! And you in rags."

"I care not for worldly comforts, Alistair. I just crave safe passage for all of us. If Archie provides that, then I am grateful."

Glenaladale waves to the rest of the men to join them.

Doctor Cameron is angry at Glenaladale's suggestions. "Come, your majesty, I want to show you what is left of the Cameron wealth."

The party is led from the waterfall along a short path that emerges into the Cameron estate at Achnacarry.

"There it is ... all that is left of the Clan Cameron."

In front of them is a large burnt-out blacked house with little more than the end walls standing. "That you will remember was Lochiel's house."

Glenaladale orders the party to rest.

"Lochiel and I were born in that house."

"I'm sorry for the mischief I have caused the Camerons."

"Tis only stone and mortar. You are flesh and blood."

Two Redcoats have been stationed on the grounds to watch for returning Jacobites. They see the Prince's large number, and make their escape.

The Glenmorrison men fire shots without effect.

"Lockhart's men. They have been patrolling here on the lookout for remnants of your army. They will be back with a whole detachment."

Glenaladale barks orders. "John! Get the men divided into small parties."

"Aye, Alistair."

The Glenaladales and the Glenmorrison men have divided into three smaller parties.

"We will meet with you at the Gairlochy crossing in three days. God speed."

Glenaladale stops him. "Bring some of that lost coin, Cameron."

Cameron bows to the Prince, moves off with Lochgarry.

Captain Glenaladale with the Chisholm's, Young Borrodale with the other Glenmorrison men except for Patrick Grant, set off in opposite directions. Major Glenaladale, Patrick Grant and the Prince make up the third party.

"Where are we going, Alistair."

He points. "Up there. From the top we will be able to see up and down the Great Glen, across Arkaig to Skye, and south beyond Ben Nevis."

The Prince, Glenaladale and Patrick are on the summit of an unnamed mountain wrapped in their plaids.

The clouds race by. The sun goes down. Summer is almost gone and a cold breeze descends on them from the north.

The Great Glen, 28th August. Doctor Cameron, Glengarry and Sandy MacPherson, their guide, are waiting with the bulk of the Glenaladale and Glenmorrison party now reunited. The last of them has waded across the Lochy river.

Cameron is anxious that the Prince has not shown up. "We cannot wait here much longer. We will be found."

John Glenaladale "My brother will be along presently with the Prince."

"No, we cannot wait a second longer. We must

disperse." Cameron indicates to Lochgarry and MacPherson that they are leaving.

Captain Glenaladale draws his pistol. "Sit back down, gentlemen."

They do as they are told.

A shout goes up.

Glenmorrison MacDonald "Tis MacCullony!"

Charles, Glenaladale and Patrick appear from a wood. The men rush forward to greet the three of them.

"Tis a joy to see you all!

Cameron "I have brought fresh funds, your highness.

"Then, give it out, Archie! A guinea a man for each week served!"

"Your highness... that is a small fortune."

"Pay them, Archie!"

"Yes, your highness."

Grant "Tis a blessing, your highness. For the men have nothing but the clothes they stand in. I thank you."

Glenaladale, his wounds now healed, is embraced by Charles. "Alistair. I am in your debt."

"T'was a fine time we had, sir."

"T'was, the best. You made a man of me."

The Glenaladales and the Glen Morrison men are lined up to a man, down on one knee, with their bonnets in their hands. Grant translates the Prince's address to them.

"Men. I salute you. I am loath to leave you. You are the finest men I have ever had under my command. When I return, may I call on your services again?"

In chorus they shout "Aye!!!"

The Prince removes his cap and bows to his men.

"Rise, gentlemen. Get you to your families and keep them safe. Farewell!"

The Prince turns from his men. MacPherson, Glengarry and Doctor Cameron lead him. The others watch as the Prince is led into the hills on the southern side of the glen.

Glenaladale is apart with Grant. "I am a ruined man, Patrick, but I would play my part again."

"Why does the Prince trust Doctor Cameron so much?

"The Prince judges a man by his service. He knows Cameron has stolen his gold, but he will let him have it in exchange for his deliverance."

"Tis a strange existence."

"Aye. There may be perfidy in that kind of life. The Prince after all is a Stuart"

The party of four has successful crossed the military road without detection. They climb past the hamlet of Roy and take the old drover road up into Glen Roy.

The Prince recognises where he is, asks Cameron for confirmation. "We came this way last year with a thousand men?"

"Indeed we did, sir, with banners flying."

"Tis a smaller party but a more valuable one we are now."

In time they turn southwards towards Loch Laggan, then across the shoulder of mighty Ben More, spending the night in a craggy shelter.

By a small shieling on Loch Ericht, Lochiel and two Cameron retainers wait patiently to greet the Prince's party as it descends the southern slope of the mountain. As the Prince's party approaches, the Prince runs and throws himself into the arms of Lochiel.

They embrace like long lost father and son. There is much rejoicing before Lochiel leads the Prince into the shieling.

The hut is small and smoky. They are eating heartily on mutton, beef sausages, butter, cheese, bacon-ham, and pints of whisky.

The Prince is about to dip his hand into a large saucepan. Lochiel hands him a silver spoon. He takes it and recalls his former self.

"Now I will eat like a prince!"

They are happy that he is happy. The Prince takes his fill, and as he settles to smoke his pipe, we wonder at the feast they have just taken.

"Are you accustomed to eating so richly, Donald?"

"MacPherson has looked after me well." He looks to his brother Archie who is uncomfortable with the conversation.

"Tis more than four months since I saw you at your house lying wounded."

"Aye, my ankles still bother me but as you see, my legs work." Lochiel feels inhibited by his brother's presence. "Archie, I have a terrible itch. Will you fetch me some clean bandages."

"Aye, Donald..." Cameron gets up and goes out.

Lochiel leans forwards and whispers. "That crazy coot MacPherson. He's utterly mad."

"With my gold?"

"Most certainly."

"The young MacDonalds as well?

"Some of the MacDonalds, aye? And my brother Archie. Cluny MacPherson is the main culprit. He's never short of a guinea despite living in a cave. You'll see for yourself when I take you there tomorrow."

The Prince is brought up the hillside to Cluny's Cage. The whole house is an egg shape, half hung, half standing in a steep hillside thicket.

The Prince is astounded at the structure. He enters with Lochiel and Doctor Cameron.

"How long has MacPherson been here, Donald?"

"Who knows? He never gives a straight answer. He is a law unto himself."

There is commotion from the back of the cave. Coming towards the Prince is Cluny MacPherson, forty years old, wild haired, and bearded to his chest.

"What is this? You're standing there without a drink in your hand. Janet! Janet!"

Janet MacPherson, twenty-eight, his wife appears. "Aye, Cluny? What's the matter now?"

"Its the Prince, woman! Get supper on!"

"Och" says Janet, gives the Prince a quick look over, then departs into the back of the cave again.

The Prince and Lochiel exchange glances. Doctor Cameron sucks on his pipe as if he's seen it all before.

Night has fallen. The Prince, Lochiel, Dr. Cameron and Cluny are sitting by a fire, drinking merrily, puffing on their cutty pipes.

MacPherson is holding court. "There I was at Dalchully House, hiding in the bolt hole in the East wing when Colonel Munro turns up, the very man charged with searching for me. See, he personally wants the one thousand pounds that's on my head. "

He grins. "Well, since we have never met, I went outside and held the Colonel's horse whilst he went inside to look for me." He turns serious. "He was a gentleman about it. When he came out, he gives me a penny for my trouble and rode off!"

Cluny roars with laughter. "And have you heard about yon Young Clanranald? What a scoundrel. Deserted he has, your highness, deserted his whole clan for Mary Hamilton. Mary Hamilton! Earl of Selkirk's daughter. His own first cousin! She's no half as braw as my Janet."

The Prince is puzzled. "You're speaking of Clanranald's son? Colonel Ranald?"

"Aye, that's him, the commander of the MacDonald's. What a grand excuse. Taking them off the field at Culloden because Murray had stuck them on the left. He got the frights, the wee coward."

"He's hardly a coward. He was the first to join me at Glenfinnan, and he went to Derby and back with us."

"Then what is he? Have you seen him this whole time since the battle? He's just like his father. Thinks only on himself. He's run off to the Continent with the Hamilton girl and some of your gold."

He stumps out his pipe. "And his poor mother? Rotting in yon HMS Furnace while they look for you up and down the length of the Highlands."

This is new information to Charles. He takes it personally.

"If you'd waited until I was finished beating the Redcoats in Atholl, I would have got my men up to Inverness, licked Cumberland's lackeys, and you'd no be in this pickle."

"That's enough, Ewen. You are speaking out of turn."

Doctor Cameron interjects. "I seem to remember, MacPherson, that I came to apprehend you last year as you were on the side of the British government."

"Well, I switched sides, didn't I. I'm a wanted man just like the rest of ye."

He raises his cup. "Here's to us that are wanted, and those that want us!"

They reluctantly drink to the toast.

Some weeks have passed and the Prince has become accustomed to his new abode. The Prince is resting, smoking his pipe, reading a London newspaper. He is no longer on every page.

Cluny comes to him with Sandy MacPherson.

"My man here says that there's a French ship anchored in Loch nan Uamh."

The Prince throws down the paper. "Come for me?

"Aye, and the others of Lochiel's ilk."

"Are you not coming with us, MacPherson?"

"Naw. Janet's with child. I'll wait for you to come back. Will that be next year or the year after?"

The Prince picks up his musket, departs.

Cluny roars with laughter.

The Prince, Lochiel, Doctor Cameron and the Cameron Retainers have set out on the long march to the coast. It is a five-day journey of weaving and backtracking back across the Great Glen, then westwards towards Borrodale, after a night at Cameron's burnt out house.

On the sixth day, the Prince's party is descending from Loch Mama in single file. As the Prince is passing an outcrop, a musket is levelled inches from his head.

The Prince stops dead. He has finally been apprehended.

The man with the musket lowers the barrel. It is Neil MacDonald. Standing with him is Captain Alex MacLeod.

"I have never been so happy to see anyone!" The Prince embraces them both as long lost friends.

"Your highness! I wasn't sure if you were an impostor."

The Prince disengages and stands back for them to admire him. "I'm Dugald MacCullony" Tis a better disguise than Betty Burke's. What do you think?" Charles bars his teeth. They are black.

Captain MacLeod "I'd take you for a Highlander any day."

"A little soot from the fire on my face and teeth. And voila!" He laughs as he always does at his own joke. "Is Ned with you?"

"I left Ned Burke in Stornoway with Captain O'Neil. O'Neil was taken in North Uist, but Ned, a Uist man himself, is said to be loose on this mainland."

Neil "He'll be looking for a new master to vex."

The Prince is animated. "It will not be me! I am my own servant now."

It is the 19th September. *L'Heureux*, a French frigate is anchored in Loch nan Uamh. There is a heavy mist sitting on the water. The Prince, Lochiel, Doctor Cameron, Glengarry, Neil MacDonald, and Alex MacLeod and being rowed to the ship.

Neil MacDonald calls out in French "Hoi?

A French voice shout back "C'est ca le Prince?"

"Oui!"

A rope is thrown down.

On deck, The Prince takes Neil's hand. "I am in your debt. You have secured my departure as you promised me on the Long Island."

Neil is modest. "Tis a small thing. We've been anchored here praying we wouldn't be blown out of the water." In French, he shouts to the Captain of the ship "The Prince is aboard! Set sail!"

Orders are given in French. The sound of the anchor being raised confirms that the ship is on its way to France.

"Excuse me, your highness. I have to brief the pilot." Neil leaves the deck and goes below.

Lochiel, Cameron and the many others aboard the ship hug one another in relief. One by one they come to Charles and kiss his hand. He is once more the master, not the servant. His companions know that they need his influence with the king to make a live for themselves in Paris as exiles.

As the ship drifts out of the shelter of the loch, The Prince looks back towards the shore.

He is silhouetted against the rising mountains towering over the loch. It is his last view of the land he has come to know so well.

He silently prays that he will see Scotland again.

THE END

AFTER THE GREAT GETAWAY

Of the characters who sacrificed everything to help the Prince, the following will suffice to give the reader comfort that their loyal assistance to the Prince was in time revered, rather than punished.

Colonel John O'Sullivan - made his escape from South Uist aboard *L'Heureux*, returned to Paris and was knighted by James III.

Captain Felix O'Neill, after capture, was taken to Edinburgh Castle, released on parole in 1747. He returned to Paris and arranged the Prince's marriage to Clementina Walkinshaw

Ned Burke - hid for many months in North Uist, escaped back to Edinburgh, took up his old job as a sedan chair man.

Old Donald MacLeod was transported to Tilbury. He was released in the 1747 amnesty, returned to Skye and died two years later.

Neil MacDonald stayed in France and married a French girl. His son Etienne became a Marshal of France, then the Duke of Taranto.

Lady Clanranald was imprisoned in Tilbury and went mad. Her husband Clanranald was arrested some months after her and imprisoned with her until July 1747.

Old MacKinnon captured at Morar's bothy was kept imprisoned with Donald MacLeod at Tilbury, released 1747, and returned to Skye to father three more children, before dying in 1756.

Captain John MacKinnon was captured at Ergol, jailed on a prison hulk at Tilbury, released in 1747, his health ruined.

Captain Donald Roy MacDonald avoided capture, became a schoolmaster in Skye, and wrote poetry in Latin.

Malcolm MacLeod, was sent to London to stand trial, but released. He became the perfect Highland gentleman. Doctor Johnston and James Boswell visited him in 1773.

The Glenmorrison men disbanded shortly afterward the Prince's departure. John MacDonald, in was in fact a Campbell. Patrick Grant pressed into Wolfe's army, served at the siege of Quebec and became a Chelsea Pensioner.

Doctor Archibald Cameron returned to Scotland in 1753 to recover the Loch Arkaig gold, but was betrayed, tried, and executed for treason, the last Jacobite to ever hang.

Cluny MacPherson - remained at Cluny's cage for eight years, joined the other exiled chiefs like Lochiel in France in 1754.

Old Kingsburgh - ended up a prisoner in Edinburgh Castle. After being released in 1747 he returned to Skye and died at the age of eighty-three.

Flora MacDonald was imprisoned in the Tower of London but became quite celebrated. In 1747 she was freed and returned to Skye escorted by Malcolm MacLeod to marry Kingsburgh's son. They emigrated to North Carolina, but she returned to Scotland in 1779 after her husband was captured fighting on the British side in the American Revolution.

Charles Edward Stuart lived in exile in France, then Italy until 1779. He never saw Scotland again and is interred with his father in the Stuart vault in St. Peter's, Rome.

ROBBIE MOFFAT

The author was born and schooled in Glasgow. He took a degree in English language and Literature at Newcastle University. He began writing when he was seventeen and has a had a career as a poet, novelist, playwright and screenwriter. He is best known for his feature film work in which he is also a director and producer.

His prose writing as been overshadowed by this. He wrote his first novel when he was twenty two and continued to write novels for the next twenty years. None of them were published.

The rediscovery of his prose work has lead to a recent spate of publications that has lead to a resurgence of interest in his prose work.